SEBASTIAN

FEDERAL PROTECTION AGENCY

BOOK SEVEN

BY EVIE RILEY

Sebastian

Federal Protection Agency

Book Seven

Copyright © 2024

Evie Riley

Second Edition

ISBN: 978-1-77357-672-5

Published by Naughty Nights Press LLC

Cover Art By Willsin Rowe

SEBASTIAN

When the past catches up,

will love be enough?

Private Investigator Sebastian Roth and his older brother have spent almost two decades protecting themselves from a bloodthirsty crime family. Until now, they've managed to stay one step ahead of the mafia cartel's goons, but it seems like the past is finally catching up.

Forced once more to hope the FBI can keep them safe after another attempt on their lives, can they trust the very authorities who let them down before? Or will the brothers have to flee all over again?

Paramedic and nursing student Newt Clary literally fell into the lap of the hottest man he's ever met. He finds a way to meet up with the tall, dark, hunky man and discovers someone who shares his love of video games. There's just something so secretive about the sexy older man, but Newt can't help wanting to know more.

When an attempt is made on his life for his connection to Sebastian, can Newt look past the secrets his new love interest has been hiding, or will it be at the risk of his own life?

Can Sebastian and Newt find a way to be together and remain safe? Or will the past tear apart any potential future?

Trigger Warnings: Death, violence, mentions of trafficking and other crimes.

CHAPTER ONE

Newt

ELLIE AND I had just finished cleaning and refilling the stock in ambulance sixty-one when the clang of the call bells rang out over the staticy PA system of Firehouse Twenty-One, followed by the address and information of the call. An abandoned warehouse fire. Should make for an easy call for her and I, at least.

Firefighters scrambled to their trucks, pulling on their fire gear and climbing into their assigned vehicles seconds before the big trucks lumbered out and raced away, sirens blaring.

"Here we go again," Ellie quipped. "No

rest for the wicked." She flashed me a grin as she slammed the back door to the bus closed, and then quickly rounded the vehicle to slide into the driver's seat as I popped my small frame up into the passenger side.

"I prefer staying busy. Makes the shift go by faster," I replied as I fit my coffee cup into the holder that Ellie slid out from the dashboard, and then popped a handful of M&Ms in my mouth, reveling in the chocolaty goodness that burst over my tongue. Hopefully the sweet treat—one I was truly addicted to—would get me by for the rest of this shift as we hadn't had a chance to grab anything to eat from the station's kitchen since breakfast this morning.

It had been back-to-back callouts today, mostly small stuff like kids getting cuts and scrapes, or a new mother going into labor with no one home to help her navigate the new and exciting experience, but we both loved it.

As I was also currently putting myself thorough nursing school, moonlighting as a paramedic was the ideal job and helped pay the bills, and I wouldn't trade my team at Station Twenty-One for any of the other stations I'd worked at. I was so thrilled when Ellie and I were offered a permanent spot at Twenty-One, as the rotation between houses had become frustrating and difficult to co-ordinate with my shifts at the hospital. The station was a block from Mercy Hospital, where I was doing my internship, and my apartment only a block farther than that, so the convenience of walking between the three was perfect.

Buckling my belt, I grabbed the sidebar of the door as Ellie flipped on the lights and whipped the bus out of the garage, heading to the address we'd been given for the call. An abandoned building fire typically didn't give us much to do in the way of providing medical care but we were on hand in case anyone nearby happened to need our help, or in the event one of the firefighters who risked their lives running in to the burning buildings needed assistance after inhaling too much smoke or in the event that they suffered an injury of some sort, as had happened to Jase Turner several months back. It was a job-related hazard, I guess.

The night was alive with the crackle of flames, painting the sky in hues of orange and red as we pulled up to the site. My pulse quickened as Ellie stopped the ambulance off to the side of Engine forty-three. Yellow and black-garbed figures dotted the blacktop as the firefighters rushed into the fray.

The wail of sirens echoed in the distance as we grabbed our gear bags from the back of the ambulance and raced toward the scene, the adrenaline coursing through my veins.

The building loomed before us, a towering inferno of flame and smoke swallowing everything in its path.

"Over here!" Hawke Colton's voice echoed from beyond the smoke and embers filling the air.

Suddenly, through the haze, I spotted Cyrus MacMillan and Quinn Sanders, two more firefighters from my station emerging from the flames, carrying a figure between them, Hawke bringing up the rear.

My heart sank as I realized it was a victim who'd obviously been trapped in the building during the blaze.

This wasn't going to be pretty.

The firefighters hurried toward us, their faces grim beneath their soot-stained masks. Without a word, they gently lowered the victim to the stretcher. The victim's clothing had all but burned away, only small scraps of remaining material trailing over parts of his body, and revealing the extent of his injuries.

But there was no time to dwell on the horror of it all. We had a job to do.

We quickly assessed the victim's injuries.

"Damn, he's bad," Ellie muttered, her voice laced with concern.

I nodded grimly, taking in the charred flesh and labored breathing of the victim.

"Let's get him stabilized and out of here," I said, my voice steady despite the chaos around us.

I knew there was no time to waste. We needed to act fast if we were going to save him.

Together, we sprang into action, our movements swift and sure.

"Airway's compromised," Ellie called out, her voice cutting through the roar of the fire. "We need to intubate."

I nodded, handing her the necessary equipment as we worked in tandem, our movements synchronized like a well-oiled machine.

Through the maze of charred skin, I managed to get a line into his foot and pushed saline, followed by a dose of morphine, hoping to ease his pain as best we could. Ellie applied saline-soaked sterile dressings to the worst of his wounds.

We gotta move," I announced. "He's not gonna last long out here."

With the victim stabilized as much as possible, we carefully loaded him into the back of the ambulance and I slid onto the jump seat, hooking up the monitors to the bus's interior power and monitoring systems so I could keep an eye on his stats easier.

Ellie closed the doors and with a double tap to the back of the bus, she hurried around and slid into the driver's seat. Cranking the engine, Ellie simultaneously spoke into the mic. "This is ambulance sixty-one, we're on route with a burn victim, ETA three minutes." Relaying the details of the status of our patient, Ellie expertly navigated the ambulance through the labyrinth of emergency vehicles filling the street and we began the short journey to the hospital.

SEBASTIAN

"Hang in there, buddy," I murmured, trying to offer some semblance of comfort to the patient as we navigated through the smoke-filled street.

It seemed like only seconds before Mercy hospital loomed before us, a beacon of hope amidst the chaos of the night. As the ambulance screeched to a halt, I could feel the weight of the victim's fate resting heavily on my shoulders.

The back doors swung open and Ellie grabbed the foot of the stretcher.

"Let's move, Newt!" Ellie's voice cut through the urgency of the moment, her eyes focused and determined.

Together, we sprang into action, unloading the stretcher with practiced efficiency. The wounded man lay motionless, his breathing shallow and labored, his blackened skin still smoldering with the remnants of the inferno that had nearly claimed his life.

The emergency room doors flew open, and a flurry of activity ensued as doctors and nurses rushed to our side.

"We've got a severe burn victim, no ID," I called out to the waiting medical team, my voice steady despite the adrenaline coursing through my veins.

With swift precision, the attending ER doctor took control, assessing the victim's condition and calling out the applicable treatments to their co-workers.

As we swiftly made our way down the short hallway, Ellie gave them a rundown of the patient's stats when he'd been delivered into our care, and our other observations during the ride over, as well as the procedures we'd followed in the field. Everything was standard protocol and we followed it without even having to really think about it.

"Trauma bay two," one of the doctors barked, his voice sharp with urgency.

As the John Doe was wheeled into the emergency room, I couldn't help but feel a surge of relief. We had done everything in our power to get him here safely, but now it was out of our hands.

"Good job, Newt," Ellie said, her voice soft with admiration as we watched the doors swing shut behind the victim.

I nodded, a sense of pride swelling in my chest. "Thanks, Ellie. You too." I flashed her a smile as we traversed back though the hospital, exiting the sliding ambulance bay doors with a swish of air behind us.

SEBASTIAN

As we made our way back to the ambulance, the evening air filled with the sounds of the bustling hospital, a reminder of the countless lives being saved within its walls.

Back in the ambulance, even as the tension of the moment began to ease and the adrenaline began to ebb, it left behind a sense of exhaustion mingled with quiet satisfaction.

Ellie and I exchanged a weary glance, the silent acknowledgment of knowing exactly how the other felt in that moment passing between us.

"Another shift on the books," she said, her voice tinged with weariness.

"Yeah," I replied, a tired smile tugging at the corners of my lips. "But we made a difference tonight. That's what counts."

"We did. Let's get back to base and get this baby cleaned up again for the next shift." Ellie flashed me a smile and nodded as she turned the key, the engine of the bus roaring to life before she pulled out into the near silent streets of Baton Rouge.

As we navigated the almost empty streets, the events of the evening played over and over in my mind. The sight of the burning building, the desperate rush to save the victim, and the hectic scene at the hospital—it was all a reminder of why we do what we do.

As the city lights blurred past, I couldn't help but feel a sense of gratitude for the opportunity to make a difference, no matter how small. Because in the end, it wasn't about the glory or recognition—it was about being there when people need us most, ready to answer the call, no matter what the night may bring. And I wouldn't change a moment of it.

CHAPTER TWO

Sebastian

"SEBASTIAN," THE STARBUCKS barista yelled out.

I swiveled my head around, my heart rate skipping a beat and then giving a one two punch in my chest. I sighed as I checked the drink placed on the counter.

Yep, it was mine.

"It's just Bastian," I said as I accepted the cup, but they'd already moved on to the next customer by then and didn't hear me.

It was just a mistake. There was no way anyone here knew my real name, though my current moniker of Bastian wasn't all that far off. Really, I shouldn't be surprised when that kind of thing happened, but I suppose all the years of being hyper-vigilant had taken their toll. Fifteen years of being hunted. Fifteen years of staying one step ahead of the potential danger with my head on a swivel and my brother at my back. Fifteen years of hiding from David Russo and his henchmen. The New Jersey Mafia Boss and his goons had been a royal pain in my ass for a long-ass time.

Really, was it any wonder I startled sometimes when someone called out my real name?

Well, at least my order was right. A flat white with hazelnut. I sighed again, my heart returning to a normal beat beneath my chest.

Stepping out onto the street holding my correct coffee, I was hit with a face full of stinging rain. Winters in Baton Rouge rarely fell below freezing since the city was so far south, but harsh rain could turn even the slightest bit of cold into a blizzard of misery.

Luckily, my long coat had a prominent collar, which I turned up to protect my neck from the rain. I clutched my coffee to my chest as I headed back to the office, hoping it would still be hot by the time I got there.

We were meeting a new client today, which always brought new headaches. I was going to need the caffeine.

The client was already there when I arrived, though they hadn't sat down yet, so I wasn't too late.

When I closed the door, I made sure to create enough noise to draw attention to myself. That was a mistake I'd made one too many times in the past. Clients didn't appreciate being startled when they were already on edge.

"Sorry. Got held up."

The client nodded, but otherwise barely paid me any attention, eyes locked on my brother, Damien. Right now he was going by Daz, the latest in his revolving list of pseudonyms.

At least his wasn't quite as close to his real name as mine was, though I knew if Russo's men looked hard enough all the name changes in the world wouldn't keep them off our tail. Still, it was just one more step in the ever-evolving plan to keep ourselves free from being unalived at the hands of that fucker.

EVIE RILEY

We'd become somewhat lax in that effort lately, even going so far as to tell our friend Mason from the Federal Protection Agency, a group of men who'd gained our trust the old-fashioned way and who we now trusted with our lives, the truth about us and our situation. Something we hadn't dared do in all the fifteen years since we watched our parents shot and killed execution style and testified against David Russo, putting him behind bars for two counts of murder in the first degree.

Most people assumed my brother was the one in charge of our firm. They weren't wrong. Damien typically gave out orders on the rare occasions when such things were necessary, and he was usually the one dealing with clients directly. However, this wasn't because he was in any way my superior. The two of us owned our PI firm, Alias Investigations, together and all decisions were a joint effort. Plus, at age thirty-four, he was only a year older than me.

No, he was not my superior. I just hated talking to people I didn't know.

Like the man sitting before us now.

According to the information we'd been

20

given earlier, the man's name was Jason Dahler.

Average looks and average height with sandy brown hair, his appearance didn't draw attention at first. However, further observation revealed a few startling details.

My years of experience as a PI had taught me to categorize clients on sight. By the time I sat down at my desk, I already had a running list in my head. There was a notch in the top of his left ear, cleanly cut like it had been sliced with a knife. The wound was old and long since healed, but it was a startling hint of violence on such an ordinary looking man.

He was also younger than I'd first thought. Exhaustion creased his face prematurely, making him look aged beyond his years. Yet, there was also a hint of concealer under his eyes. He was aware of his tired state and put in the effort to hide it. People didn't hide things without a reason. Either the man was incredibly vain, or he felt threatened and didn't want to appear vulnerable.

Altogether, the man's appearance spoke of desperation.

Dahler wasn't coming to us because he had a strong lead on whatever problem he needed fixed, but because he had no other choice. That meant more trouble for us, and even more headaches.

I looked over at Damien sitting at his own desk and he gave me a slight nod. He'd noticed the same things I had.

Leaning back in my chair, I took a sip of my already lukewarm coffee and gave our client my full attention.

"So, tell us what brings you here today, Mr. Dahler," Damien inquired, his pen poised above an old style yellow legal notepad. Yes, he truly still used the paper and pen method for recording pertinent details our clients revealed in conversation, while I was more the type to just sit back and listen while they talked and then later add a summary to the file on the computer. Not that Damien didn't use the technology or had any issue with it, he simply liked the sound of the pen scratching on the paper and the simplicity of taking notes that way. Meh, to each his own. Who was I to judge?

"It's my brother, Clay," Dahler began. "He's been missing for nearly a decade. I've spent years looking for him, I even had another PI on his case for a while but they found nothing concrete. Anyway, I think he might be somewhere in this city as that's the last bit of potentially useful information they may have found. I just can't find him. That's why I'm here. I need your help to find him and bring him home. Friends of yours from Gaithersburg recommended your investigation firm as the best in the business, and since your business just happens to be here, in the same city, it made sense anyway."

I already knew what my brother was going to say, even before he leaned forward on his desk and laced his fingers together in a contemplative pose.

"That is an incredibly vague statement, Mr. Dahler. Can you give us a little more information to go on? How did your brother disappear, for instance? Or, what makes you think he is in Baton Rouge?"

Dahler tapped his fingers nervously against each other like he was counting his words in his head. "I don't know how Clay disappeared. We just woke up one morning and he was gone. Nothing was missing and there was no sign of a break in. Nothing. He was just *gone*."

That was an incredibly unhelpful

answer. Not only did it give them nowhere to start, but it lacked details. This man wasn't reliving a painful memory. He was reciting a story.

As Damien continued interrogating the tired looking man—receiving less and less helpful answers with each question—I flipped through the information we already had in the file about this client. A lack of details in a story could be a sign of someone lying, but it could also have another cause.

Ah, there it was. Jason Dahler was just seventeen when his brother disappeared. That's the age where kids generally start to feel that they need to be adult about things, while they still very much have the feeling of being children and an unconscious desire to remain a child as long as possible. He probably felt like it was his fault somehow when his brother suddenly disappeared, and his family would have likely unintentionally fed into that guilty feeling with all their focus being on finding the brother and pretty much ignoring Jason while they did so. To him, it probably felt like it was his all fault, like he should have or could have done something to prevent his brother's kidnapping.

Quickly scanning over the information, another detail caught my eye that nearly made me drop my coffee.

Clay Dahler was the younger of the two brothers.

"How old was your brother when he disappeared?" I suddenly asked.

Dahler stared at me with a startled expression, mouth gaping like a fish for a moment as he struggled to form words. People tended to forget I was in the room when my brother took over a conversation, so when I did speak it usually startled them. I'd had people in the past compare the unexpected sound of my voice to suddenly hearing the furniture speak.

I tried not to take offence, but seriously, people treated silence like an abnormality. As if there was something wrong with me just because I didn't feel the need to constantly fill the air with words.

Raising one eyebrow, I took another sip of my coffee and waited for Mr. Dahler to answer. Hopefully, he heard my question the first time, because I wouldn't be repeating myself.

"Oh, um, right." Dahler shook his head to chase away the shock and managed to find his voice again. "Clay was fourteen when he disappeared. He'd be twenty-three now. Old enough to drink. I never thought he'd be gone long enough to miss that milestone."

Hmm, not as young as I'd originally thought but still young enough nonetheless. I frowned but didn't say anything else and let my brother continue with his line of questioning.

Dahler's wording bothered me.

Gone.

Not missing. *Gone.*

That word almost made it sound like Clay Dahler had just decided to leave one day, and his continued absence was his own fault. No child just up and left home on their own unless there was some very nasty reason they didn't want to be there, and that wasn't the feeling I got in this case.

I wasn't sure if Jason Dahler was hiding something important that he simply couldn't handle admitting to, or if he refused to use the word "taken" so he wouldn't have to face reality, but either way, I didn't predict a good outcome for this job.

CHAPTER THREE

Sebastian

DAMIEN'S FIST HIT my stomach, causing me to double over as the air suddenly left my lungs. The position put me off balance, and he used the opportunity to sweep my feet out from under me. My back hit the ground with a harsh thud, and before I could even take a breath, he was kneeling over me with one knee on my chest and his hand at my throat.

He smiled down at me. "You're dead. That's the third time I've killed you today."

"Yeah, yeah," I grumbled, slapping his hand away. "You win. You don't have to gloat about it."

Almost every important conversation Damien and I ever exchanged happened while sparring. Something about the movement of our fists made the difficult words flow easier. Any time one of us had something to say, we dragged the other off to our little homemade gym on the residential floor above the office, which I'd moved into when Damien had bought a new place with his partners recently. Not that he'd expected me to move away from him, we'd always lived together over our fifteen years on the run, but I did it because being around the three of them as they were all lovey dovey and having sex all the time wasn't my bag. It just made more sense for me to live in the apartment above the firm, even if it was rather small. I didn't need much space, after all.

Creating the gym upstairs meant taking space away from the rest of the apartment, too—the bedrooms barely had enough space for double beds and the kitchen was basically just a cluster of appliances in one corner—but it was worth the sacrifice. I'd take training, sparring, and talking with my brother over the luxury of more space any day. Especially since we rarely saw one another outside of work these days.

Once assured of his victory, Damien sat on the floor next to my shoulder. One elbow balanced on his knee while his other hand stroked his newly re-grown beard.

Damien had a unique talent for keeping his short beard perfectly groomed. Not a hair stood out of place, even after our sparring match. The sharp line it created along his jaw rivaled the edge of the finest blade. It was an impressive sight. It was also an obvious giveaway to anyone who knew him well. When Damien's hand went to his chin, beard or no beard stroking, that meant he had something on his mind. So, I didn't bother to get up and just reclined on the mat as I waited for him to find the right words.

Less than a minute passed before he spoke.

"You seem agitated. Something about that client bothered you."

I shrugged, though the action probably looked awkward from a prone position. "Not bothered, just... brothers, you know.

One of them missing. The other desperately looking for him. Clay Dahler was only fourteen when he disappeared. No fourteen-year-old kid goes missing suddenly for innocent reasons. You and I both know he's probably dead by now. Even if he isn't, and we do manage to find him, the condition he's likely to be in is… well, not good. It all just reminds me of how easily that could have been us."

A memory passed behind my eyes, so fast it was barely more than a blur of color.

Voices arguing.

The bright light of a muzzle flash, followed by the reverberation of a gun firing, and finally, the horrible sound of absolute silence.

Hiding in the closet with my brother's hand pressed tightly over my mouth, holding in the petrified sobs that threatened to escape my chest.

Slowly making our way down the stairs to the living room, fear of the gunman and his goons still being there or coming back for us despite the fact we knew we'd heard them leave.

The sight of bright red blood staining the white carpet only inches from my shoe.

I shook my head, pushing the memories back.

Damien sat in silence for a moment, before finally blurting out, "I've noticed that you haven't been taking on as many cases lately. If you're not interested in being a PI anymore, or if all the stuff we see is starting to bother you, I won't mind if you quit to pursue something else. You know that, right?"

I shot up off the floor and sat directly in front of my brother, kneeling with my knees folded awkwardly under me.

"No, it's nothing like that. It's because..."

I hesitated.

What could I tell him?

I didn't want to lie to my brother, but I had to tell him something.

"I don't want to quit. I like that we help people. This one just got under my skin because it's a pair of brothers. I'm sorry if I seemed distant lately. I promise, I'll be more involved from now on."

The knowledge in his eyes cut right through me as Damien scowled. He'd definitely noticed my hesitation, but to my relief he chose not to point it out.

"Fine," he relented with a sigh. "Since

it affects you like this, I'll take point on the Dahler case. However, we might be able to wrap it up quickly. I got a report earlier from a hospital nearby of a John Doe that matches Clay's description."

I scoffed and rolled my eyes. "Too easy. What are the odds that the person we're looking for would turn up just hours after we get the case? Besides, we aren't even sure the man is even in this city. Jason Dahler was quite vague about the details of how he actually tracked his brother here."

Standing up, Damien offered me a hand off the floor. "I know. I would have dismissed it too, except Clay Dahler has a distinctive birthmark on the inside of his wrist, and this John Doe has a similar mark."

I accepted his helping hand and stood as well, brushing dust from my black jeans. "Similar? Shouldn't it be exact?"

"Apparently, the John Doe was burned, so it's hard to tell. We'll have to take a look for ourselves, but I'm busy today. Our contacts at the FBI have requested another meeting."

Groaning, I tipped my head back so far, my eyes pointed toward the ceiling.

We needed to dust the ceiling fan. Spiders were starting to make nests behind the light bulbs.

"What do they want? Another case they can't solve that they're going to push onto us?"

My relationship with the FBI was rocky, at best. It was a memory I tried not to think about too often. To put it simply, our parents had been killed. My brother and I saw it happen, and testified against David Russo, the mafia leader, in court, putting ourselves at risk for the sake of justice. The FBI had put us into witness protection and promised to protect us.

They failed.

We only survived by going into hiding on our own, changing our last names and reinventing ourselves on the other side of the country.

Ever since then, I couldn't help but view the FBI as an extension of the villain that haunted our lives. If they'd just done their job right the first time, Damien and I wouldn't have had to live in fear for so many years. Maybe we wouldn't have had to watch our parents die at all.

That was one of the things I liked best about my job now. As a private investigator, I could pick up where organizations like the FBI failed.

Damien shoved me toward the door. "Hey, they pay us, so what does it matter? However, I do need to meet with them, and then I need to meet up with Mason at the FPA office for another case, so you'll have to check out the John Doe. It's probably not our guy, but this way we can at least cross it off the list."

I nodded even before my mouth formed the words. "Yeah. Of course I'll go. Give me the details and I'll leave right now."

No further explanation was required. When Damien needed something done, I did it, and when I needed something, he always came through. There was no other option. After everything we'd been through together, relying on each other came as easily as breathing.

Maybe that was why keeping secrets from my brother felt like drowning.

CHAPTER FOUR

Sebastian

IF SOMEONE WERE to read a summary of my life on paper, they would probably expect me to have some sort of trauma regarding hospitals. Parents murdered by the mafia. Hunted down by that same mafia. Now working as a private investigator with both the FBI and the newly developed FPA task force.
Surely that meant I'd experienced my fair share of injuries, right?

Well, injuries yes. Hospitals, not so much.

Spending so many years in hiding, Damien and I had learned to take care of the majority of physical wounds on our own. Things were better now. We could seek medical help without fear of discovery, but such instincts were ingrained into us so deeply, no amount of time could ever iron it all out.

All that was to say, I couldn't remember the last time I set foot in a hospital. It was more chaotic than I expected. People were constantly moving around, machines beeped just out of sight, and staticy announcements blared from the PA system every few minutes.

I observed it all with wary curiosity as I sat on a hard chair in the waiting room. The John Doe I was there to visit was apparently kept in a special secluded ward where people couldn't just wander in. I needed someone to take me there, but no one seemed in a hurry to do so. Half an hour had passed with nothing to do but read outdated magazines before someone finally called my name.

"Bastian Roth?"

I looked up as my moniker was called out. Freckles and blue eyes filled my vision. A young man dressed in scrubs stood before me with a bright smile on his face. He had red hair—properly ginger, not the auburn color that people often called red—and a pale complexion that made every freckle on his nose and cheeks stand out in stark contrast.

It was like he had a constellation on his face. For a moment I was envious. This man carried his own lucky stars with him wherever he went.

Too late, I realized the sound of my name had been a question and I hadn't answered.

Confusion dimmed the man's smile. "Are you not Bastian Roth? The front desk pointed me toward you, but maybe they were wrong."

Clearing my throat, I stood and tried to look confident, like I hadn't just made such a stupid blunder as forgetting to respond to the name.

"That's me."

"Great." The smile was back, even brighter than before. "I'm nurse Clary, but you can just call me Newt. Everyone does. You're here about the John Doe, right? I can take you to see him. Follow me."

There was no time to reply before the nurse was already walking away. I hurried to follow. If I got lost in this labyrinth of hallways, I would never find my way out without a guide.

Newt?

It was an odd name, probably short for something else, but appropriately cute. Everything about the man was cute. He was small in stature, both in height and width. There was nearly a foot of difference between us, and his steps barely seemed to touch the linoleum floor when he walked. Red hair hung just long enough to touch his chin. Most of it had been pulled back into the smallest ponytail I had ever seen, like a pompom on the back of his head. However, a few locks at the front didn't reach the ponytail and were instead kept out of his face by a pair of barrettes.

Even his scrubs were cute, covered in a colorful Pac-Man design. I hadn't played the game in a while, but I knew how it worked. Instinctually, my gaze traveled down his clothes, plotting out a course through the printed maze that would allow me to collect the most dots and cherries while avoiding ghosts.

It wasn't until I found myself staring at the other man's ass that I realized what I was doing. I'd just been ogling this nurse for several minutes. My thoughts had been innocent, but no one else would know that. From the outside, I probably looked like a letch.

My ears burned hot with embarrassment. I looked away, quickly glancing around to see if anyone had noticed my inappropriate behavior. No one glared at me, so hopefully not, but that was no guarantee.

I sped up so Newt and I walked side by side. This change in position seemed to inspire conversation, for the other man immediately started talking.

"I actually brought this John Doe in a few days ago. It was a warehouse fire. Pretty bad. Hopefully, you can give us some info about his identity. He'll need support to recover, and I hate that he's just lying here alone."

I could feel blue eyes looking up at me, but I kept my gaze carefully pointed forward. "Brought him in?"

"Oh, yeah, I, um..." Newt nervously scratched at his temple, dislodging one of the barrettes so it hung crooked. "I'm a paramedic at Firehouse Twenty-One. We were the ones who responded to the fire, and I'm the one who brought this John Doe to the hospital."

As we stopped at one of the many identical doors, I considered Newt again.

"You don't look like a paramedic. How can you do that and be a nurse?"

If anything, he looked like he should be working with kids. Maybe as a preschool teacher or a nanny. From what I knew about paramedics and nurses, both seemed like difficult jobs.

Where did he find enough hours in the day?

He stopped with his hand on the handle of the door. "Yeah, I get that a lot." He laughed, but it didn't sound happy. "However, I passed all the physical requirements, so don't worry about that. Plus, I'm just a nursing assistant. Not a fully registered nurse. So I only work here part time."

Had I said something wrong?

Newt seemed uncomfortable, twisting at the hem of his scrubs in his free hand like he was wringing them dry. That was a clear sign of nervousness, but I couldn't see anything he had to be nervous about.

Damien often accused me of having a mean *resting-bitch-face*. When I wasn't actively trying to express an emotion, my face naturally settled into a shape that made it look like I was scowling. Along with my size, and my habit of remaining quiet around people I didn't know, it apparently made for an intimidating combination.

Hoping to relieve the tension that had developed between us, I flashed him an awkward smile. "Having two jobs is still impressive. I can barely handle one some days."

The smile sat awkwardly on my face. Too much of my teeth showed. I felt like a bad imitation of the Cheshire cat. However, my effort worked well enough for Newt to stop fidgeting and finally open the door.

Inside the room, the man lying on the bed barely looked human. There were so many bandages and wires coming off him, I couldn't even tell it was a man. I would have to trust the hospital staff's judgment that this was a John Doe and not a Jane Doe.

"He hasn't woken up yet, thankfully," Newt said as he stepped around to the head of the bed. "If he was awake, we'd have to sedate him, anyway. Almost eighty percent of his body has been burned."

EVIE RILEY

I could feel my face shutting down and my expression reverted to its neutral scowl. It was what I always did when I didn't know how to react. This wasn't the first time I'd seen someone injured. It wasn't even the worst injury I'd seen, but I'd never figured out a good way to react.

What could one possibly say in the face of such tragedy?

"I'm sorry," would never be enough.

Instead, I pressed forward and focused on my job.

"I'll need to see his left wrist. There's supposed to be a birthmark there. If this is the guy I'm looking for anyway."

Newt very carefully turned the man's wrist over, making sure not to disrupt the bandages or the IV.

I stepped over to the side of the bed, holding out my phone with the info that Damien had sent me. The man had a birthmark, but it had been partially destroyed by burns and what little remained was distorted.

Jason Dahler had given us some photos of his brother's birthmark. It looked like a seahorse. Such a unique mark should be easily identifiable. However, the picture was from when Clay

44

was twelve years old. The mark could have changed as he grew.

Shaking my head, I stored my phone back in my coat. "There are some similarities between the marks, but it's not enough for me to say that this is definitely Clay Dahler."

Newt tucked the patient's arm back under the covers. "I'm sorry I can't offer more help. I'd like to figure out who this man is as well. We've already run his DNA, but nothing came up. Once he heals more we hope to run his fingerprints through the channels but for now the burns are simply too severe to get any prints."

I crossed my arms over my chest as I thought. Since I was already here, I wasn't going to walk away without exploring all options.

"DNA? Is it possible to run another DNA test? This time comparing it to someone else? I was hired by a man to find his lost brother. If this John Doe is related to my client, then that would give us both our answers."

"I'd have to ask the hospital's administrator for permission, but it shouldn't be a problem. Let me page them and see."

The administrator in question turned out to be on the other side of the building, and would need to talk to me in person, which meant more waiting. This time, I was directed to a private waiting room just a few doors down. Newt came with me, and I took the opportunity to probe him for more information about the warehouse fire where the John Doe had been found.

The little nurse slash EMT was happy to talk, but unfortunately didn't know much. He'd arrived after the John Doe had been pulled out of the building, and there was nothing interesting about the man's injuries other than the severity of the burns. The only thing of note that he could tell me was a theory that the warehouse fire might have been set deliberately, but even that hadn't been confirmed.

Overall, I was going to be left with nothing to show for a day of work.

I groaned and ran my fingers through my hair, feeling them catch on a few strands. My hair wasn't particularly long, but it had just enough wave to easily tangle.

Noticing my frustration, Newt offered to get me a drink and stepped over to the little refreshment table at the side of the room. Since it was a hospital, there wouldn't be anything stronger than juice, which was a shame. I could use a shot of whiskey or a few fingers of scotch right now.

There was no telling how long I'd have to wait for the administrator to arrive, so I claimed one of the room's cheap plastic seats. The nearest one had its back facing the door, so I turned it around and moved it to the left side of the doorway. This was the safest position in any room, facing the door on the side of the door hinges. Anyone entering the room wouldn't be able to see me around the body of the door, but I would be able to see them. That crucial moment of visibility could be the difference between life or death in an emergency.

I had barely sat down when Newt turned away from the refreshment table with a cup of apple juice in one hand and his phone in the other. Whatever he was looking at must have been bad news, for he swiped his thumb frantically across the screen, and with each new thing he saw his frown deepened.

Distracted as he was, he must not have noticed me move the chair. A flash of shock crossed his face as his foot made contact with my leg. Both the phone and the juice went flying and he tumbled forward into my lap.

"Sorry. So, sorry," he muttered as he fumbled to right himself without touching me. That mostly just resulted in a lot of ineffective squirming.

I wanted to comfort him and say it was okay. I didn't mind, and the apple juice had mostly landed on the floor, leaving only the bottom cuff of my pants wet. However, I said nothing. The sudden surprise of the full weight of another human being sitting on me had made me lock my jaw in place. All I could do was grab his shoulders and sit him upright, so he at least stopped writhing around.

"What is going on?"

An unexpected voice caused both Newt and I to freeze. A woman I'd never seen before stood in the doorway, her arms crossed and brows drawn into a deep frown behind square glasses.

Upon sight of her, Newt jumped to his feet, nearly tripping over me again.

"Miss Constella. I was just helping this visitor with, um, well, you know, the John Doe. He knows him. Or, actually, he knows the man's brother. Maybe. We still aren't sure. It might not be him. But, that's what I called you about. To find out."

So many words fell out of the cute little nurse all at once. Half of his sentences were practically indecipherable. He kept babbling until he ran out of breath, then fell silent with his face burning as bright red as his hair.

The woman, who I assumed was the hospital administrator I needed to speak with, just sighed and pinched the bridge of her nose.

"Nurse Clary, please get back to your duties. I'll take it from here."

"Right. Yes. Of course." He bobbed his head, like he almost wanted to bow to her then redirected himself at the last moment. With one last glance back at me, he disappeared out the door and closed it behind him.

The woman sighed again and fixed her glasses back into place.

"Sorry for the trouble," she said and held out her hand to me. "I'm Madine

Constella, the administrator for this hospital."

Just as I stood to take her hand, the door opened again, and Newt slunk back inside.

"Sorry. I just need to get..." he trailed off and pointed absently at the far corner. Giving both myself and the woman a wide berth, he crept to the other side of the waiting room and crouched down on the floor to retrieve his phone from under a chair.

"All right, I got it." He waggled the phone in the air to show it off, then seemed to realize what he was doing and quickly stowed it in his pocket. "Okay. Sorry. I'll just go. Bye." As abruptly as he reappeared, he disappeared again.

Miss Constella sighed even louder.

"Mr. Roth. You wanted to ask about a DNA test?"

This time there were no more interruptions, but that didn't make the process any easier. Apparently, having a DNA test done on someone I wasn't related to and didn't have any legal authority over was more complicated than anticipated. Not impossible, thankfully, but it required a lot more paperwork and red tape than I typically handled. Plus, I had to get in contact with Jason Dahler so the hospital could get a DNA sample from him so there would be something to compare.

These kinds of things were usually Damien's job, and despite being thirty-three years old, I felt like a child pretending to be a grown-up as I struggled to sort everything out.

An hour later, the DNA test was finally ordered with a promise that the results would be available within a few days. All I could do was give them my phone number, then go home and wait.

So, that's what I did.

CHAPTER FIVE

Sebastian

DAMIEN WASN'T THERE when I returned to the office so I re-locked the outer door and climbed the stairs to my apartment. I took a moment to change out of my apple juice stained pants and then threw myself on the couch. Without Damien there, I could sprawl over all of the cushions, my head propped up on one arm of the couch and my feet propped up on the other.

When he got back, Damien would undoubtedly want to hear about my trip to the hospital, not that I had much to tell him, so I passed the time by playing games on my phone.

My addiction to video games was one of the few things my brother didn't know about me. It didn't matter what game. From stupid little phone games to mainstream console games, I played them all. They were a great way to unwind at the end of the day and make my brain shut up for a while. As long as I was concentrating on the challenge in front of me, I wasn't thinking about anything else.

Blue eyes and freckles still filled my thoughts, so I pulled up a retro version of Pac-Man and started working my way through the levels. I had progressed through the first fifteen stages by the time I heard the front door unlock.

Before Damien could trudge up the stairs to open the door and see what I was doing, I shut off my phone and shoved it in my pocket.

It wasn't that I was embarrassed by my hobby—well, maybe a little—but I liked having something innocent that was only mine. If Damien knew that I liked video games, then he'd ask me about them and I'd feel compelled to answer. Video games were the thing I did when I was tired of talking and dealing with people. I didn't want them to be the cause of more conversation.

A moment later, Damien's familiar face peered at me over the back of the couch. "Hey, Giraffe. Move your legs."

Making a show of grumbling and taking as long as I possibly could to sit up, I created room for him on the couch.

"So, how'd it go at the hospital?" he asked once he sat down.

"Nothing yet. The John Doe's burns were too extensive to identify him at the moment. They're running a comparative DNA test on him and will get back to me. What about you? What'd the FBI want?"

Leaning back against the couch, Damien sighed.

"They've got a new case they want us and the FPA to consult on."

I could tell just from the tone of his voice that I wasn't going to like what came next.

"Actually, it's an old case that's been going on for several years. Someone has been going around the country castrating pedophiles. They aren't sure if it's a single person, or a group of people, but there have been over a dozen victims so far in Baton Rouge alone."

I snorted and didn't bother hiding the

sneer that pulled at my face. A pedophile could never be a victim. They gave up that right the minute their hands wandered where they shouldn't.

Even without saying anything, Damien knew what I was thinking and gave his own sad laugh. "Yeah. I know. But that's kind of the problem. Technically, it's still a crime, so the FBI can't just let it go, but stopping someone who's punishing pedophiles will also make them seem like the bad guys. It'll look bad no matter what they do."

"So, the FBI want us to be the bad guys for them? We catch the criminal while they keep their hands clean."

"Basically. Of course, they didn't phrase it that way. It's not something we need to worry about right now. They still don't know much. Today's consultation was just to get us up to speed on the case, so we're ready if they need to bring us in."

"Sounds like we've got nothing to do for the next few days but wait for information."

"Yep." Damien turned to me with a smile. "Max is away on a case and Travis is working late so I don't need to run home anytime soon. Want to order some dinner and put on a movie? I'll let you pick this time."

That was an opportunity I wasn't going to squander, and I quickly selected a title to watch before he could change his mind.

Damien and I agreed on most things, except when it came to movies. He liked traditional action films, with plenty of explosions, car chases, and fist fights to keep adrenaline pumping high.

I, on the other hand, hated anything with violence in it. We had enough violence in our daily lives. I didn't need it in my fictional escape as well. That severely limited my choices, especially among adult movies, so I usually ended up watching something meant for kids. I had seen every Disney movie so many times that I had all the songs memorized.

Except for The Little Mermaid. That movie I had turned off after the first few minutes and vowed never to watch again.

I really hated that singing crab.

CHAPTER SIX

Newt

IT WAS SUPPOSED to be my day off. At that moment, I should have been playing video games or sleeping, but the Firehouse where I worked the ambulance had been short staffed and called me in to cover an extra shift.

So, there I was, helping a man who had been stabbed in the leg. The man was an amateur metalworker and set up a workshop in his garage as a hobby. One of his machines had broken, sending an iron rod piercing through his thigh. The fire department had been called to literally cut the man off his machine, and then I was left to patch him up and transport him to the hospital.

At least, that's how it should have happened. When I'd arrived, the man and his wife had been arguing with the firefighters about whether to pull the metal rod out or leave it in. Luckily, they hadn't tried anything yet, but when I stepped in to take over medical care, they started arguing with me. It took me ten minutes to convince them that, yes, I was in fact a paramedic. My short stature and young face didn't inspire confidence in patients. It was an argument I had suffered through many times before, and could practically repeat in my sleep.

Once I'd convinced them that I was actually a paramedic, my next task was to explain why I wasn't going to pull the metal rod out. The object had pierced all the way down to the bone. Pulling it out would only do more damage, and likely cause more bleeding.

Eventually, I was able to secure the rod with tape and bandages and load the injured man into the ambulance to take him to the hospital. It was a job that should have taken five minutes but ended up taking half an hour due to the delays.

SEBASTIAN

When the ambulance finally started moving, I breathed a sigh of relief.

Sitting in the back of the vehicle, surrounded by medical supplies, I reminded myself that it wasn't the man's fault. He didn't know any better, and he wasn't delaying me on purpose. He was just in pain and worried, as anyone would be with a six inch piece of metal stuck in their leg.

At least one good thing came out of the delay. The man and his wife had spent so much time arguing with me, that by the time I handed the man off to the nurses at the hospital, my paramedic shift at the Firehouse was over. I could finally go home and restart my day off, only twelve hours later than it should have been.

At least the Firehouse had offered to change my schedule, so I still got a full day off. As much as I loved helping people, video games were waiting for me. I had several new titles I wanted to play and finally a few free hours to play them.

Before leaving the hospital, however, I first decided to check up on the John Doe patient.

I noticed something had changed even before I reached the private room. There were more nurses bustling around the area, and as I approached the open door, I even saw a doctor examining the John Doe. The last shift I'd worked at the hospital, the John Doe's room had practically been a ghost town. No one went in there unless they absolutely had to. After all, there was no reason to devote extra time to a patient that never changed, never moved, and probably wouldn't even wake up.

As another nurse rushed by, I grabbed her arm to catch her attention.

"What's going on? Did something happen with the patient?"

She barely paid me any attention, looking up just long enough to recognize me as a fellow staff member before mumbling a quick explanation.

"The patient has finally showed some reaction. He's not awake yet, but he has spoken. There might be a chance for him to recover."

She was gone before I could ask any further questions.

Standing awkwardly in the doorway, I watched the doctor examining the John Doe. Right before my eyes, just as the doctor touched the John Doe's face, the burned man opened his mouth and let out a yell.

"Meehaw!"

The sound was raspy, and not actually that loud despite all the effort that had been put into it. Just as quickly as the John Doe responded, he fell still once again. Neither the doctor nor any of the other nurses looked surprised, so I assumed this reaction had happened before.

Meehaw?

What did it mean?

It didn't sound like anything in English.

Spanish, maybe?

The word almost sounded like *Mija*, a Spanish endearment for girl or daughter.

Could the John Doe have a daughter?

If that was true, then we definitely needed to figure out his identity.

My spiraling thoughts were interrupted by the sudden sound of my name being called out by someone behind me.

"Nurse Clary, you're not on duty today."

I spun around to see Administrator Constella standing just behind me with her typical stern expression etched on her face.

"No, I'm not on duty today, but I was here for something else, and I just wanted to see how the patient was doing. Sorry. I'll get out of the way."

Something that could almost have been called a smile twitched the corners of her lips. "Actually, this is convenient. The DNA test for our John Doe came in. I need you to call Mr. Roth and give him the information."

She handed me a file, which I automatically accepted before I'd fully processed her words. "Of course, I... wait, what? You mean Bastian Roth, the guy who was in here a few days ago? You want me to call him?"

Her heels clicked on the linoleum floor as she walked away. "Everyone's very busy dealing with this new development, as you can see. It'll only take you a few minutes, so handle it on your own. All the information should be in there, including the phone number."

Then she was gone, and I was left standing alone in the hallway. My mouth gapped like a dying fish, trying to form words that never came.

Eventually, I managed to pull myself

together enough to stumble out of the hospital. I rode the bus all the way back to my apartment, clutching the file with one hand while pouring M&M's into my mouth with the other. Luckily, I always had a bag or two on me. No day was complete without chocolate, and in that moment, it was the only thing keeping me sane.

When I opened the door to my apartment, I was desperately glad to find my roommate, Frankie, already home. I stood in the doorway, still dressed in my scrubs with the file held out on front of me like a bomb about to blow up.

Frankie looked up from where he was cooking in the kitchen.

"Hey, Newt. How was..." As soon as his gaze landed on me, his smile fell. "Oh, no. What happened?"

"Mayday." I held the file up a little higher. "Frankie. It's a disaster. I'm going to die."

With all the patience of a god, Frankie took a seat on the couch and patted the spot next to him. "You're not going to die. Tell me what happened."

I tripped twice as I kicked off my shoes, let my jacket fall to the floor, then collapsed on the couch. Frankie's lap became my pillow as I lay on my back, staring up at the ceiling with the file clutched to my chest.

I first met Frankie in college, where we'd shared a dorm room, and we'd been friends ever since. We even pursued similar careers, though he focused on physical therapy. It was a running joke between us that we were medical bookends. When someone got hurt, I was the first person they saw, and he was the last.

After years of friendship, Frankie knew exactly how to handle me when I was in panic mode. One of his hands ran through my hair, taking out the hair tie and the barrettes that kept everything in place.

I kept meaning to get a haircut, but I could never find the time.

"Okay, what's the problem?" Frankie asked when he'd dropped the last barrette on the side table. "The world isn't ending, so it can't be that bad."

I groaned and slapped the file against my face. "It may as well be ending. You remember that guy I told you about the other day?"

SEBASTIAN

Frankie tipped his head to the side, dark eyes looking down at me with curiosity. "We each see a lot of patients every day. You'll have to be more specific."

With my face still pressed against the paper surface of the file, I mumbled as quietly as I could. "The PI who came in for the John Doe."

"Oh." Frankie's eyes lit up. "You mean the hot guy you accidentally gave a lap dance to."

The screech that came out of me could have rivaled a howler monkey as I slapped Frankie with the file. Then, when that wasn't enough, I started hitting him with every pillow I could find.

"That's. Not. What. Happened. I. Just. Fell."

His laughter could be heard even through the barrage of pillows. "Yeah, right onto his lap. Ride 'em, cowboy."

By then, I'd run out of pillows and had no choice but to try and bury myself under the couch cushions so I could die of shame. "You're impossible. Why do I tell you anything?"

"Because my advice always works. Now, sit up and tell me. Did something else happen with Mister Not-So-Private

Dick?"

Giving Frankie one more withering glare, which had no effect, I took a deep breath and rescued the file from where it had fallen to the floor. "The DNA test for the John Doe came in. Miss Constella says she's too busy to call him, which, I guess is true. But now I've been asked to contact Bastian... I mean, Mr. Roth, and tell him the results."

As he listened to my problems, Frankie twirled a piece of his hair around his finger. Unlike me, he'd grown his hair out intentionally. Dozens of shoulder length braids hung from his head. When he was working, he tied the braids back in a loose ponytail, but at home he preferred to keep them unbound. He also usually dressed in lighter colors since they contrasted with his dark skin. Altogether, it gave him a relaxed, bohemian vibe that I usually found comforting.

His patients liked him as well. They all sang his praises, and no one ever questioned Frankie about whether he was actually a physical therapist. He looked like he belonged at his job.

"Okay," Frankie said when I'd finished unleashing my woes. "Not seeing a problem here. If anything, it sounds great. You've got the perfect excuse to call the guy and ask him out to dinner."

I smacked Frankie again, with much less force this time. "I can't do that."

"No, you're right. Probably better to start with coffee. Work your way up to dinner."

"Would you be serious for a moment?" I was half tempted to throw the file across the room but stopped myself. That wouldn't be very professional.

Not that anything I'd done since getting the file could be called professional, but I had to draw the line somewhere.

"Forget speaking face to face. How can I even call the guy after doing something so embarrassing? I'll probably explode the moment I hear his voice."

I regretted my choice of words the moment I noticed a spark in Frankie's eye. The man was gearing up for another innuendo, and I quickly cut him off.

"Don't. I can see your thoughts. Get your mind out of the gutter and help me."

Frankie frowned for a moment, but relented, and the teasing glint in his eyes turned serious. "I don't think it's as bad as you're making it out to be. You had a klutzy moment. Some guys like klutzy. They think it's charming. I've even pretended to trip a few times to get a guy's attention."

That was a lie. Frankie never needed to try so hard to get someone's attention. With his flawless complexion and charming personality, people easily flocked to him. However, there was no way to say such a thing without sounding bitter, so I kept the thought to myself. Usually, it didn't bother me how much easier Frankie found the whole dating process. In the end, he'd had just as many boyfriends as I had, which was exactly none. We were both too busy with our hectic jobs to focus on much else.

The difference between us just chaffed a little after I'd made such a fool of myself in front of someone so attractive. I wished I could laugh it off as easily as Frankie did.

"No way." I shook my head. "Some people might think klutzy is cute, but not this guy. He's far too..."

I vaguely waved my hands in front of me, trying to capture the shape of everything that was Bastian Roth. The man had a constant air of intensity about him, even when he wasn't doing anything, and when he looked me in the eye, I thought my organs had melted.

He was tall too, and obviously strong. I'd gotten a good feel of the muscle under his clothes when I'd fallen on him. The man could easily pick me up, hold me against the wall and...

Nope. I stopped that train of thought before it even started. Now was not the time to get distracted by hormones.

"There's just no way. I'll call him, tell him what he needs to know, then hang up. Two minutes. Maybe less. Then it's done."

I expected Frankie to argue more, but instead he sighed and stood from the couch. Confused, I watched him leave in silence, only for him to return a moment later and hand me a small piece of paper.

"All right. I didn't want to have to do this, but I'm turning in one of my coupons."

"What? No, you can't do that."

I snatched the paper from him. Handwritten on it were the words 'Anything Coupon'. We first started exchanging these coupons back during our college days, when we were too broke to afford proper birthday or Christmas presents. We didn't need them anymore, and mostly kept them around for the sake of nostalgia, but we still honored the promise behind them.

"We're supposed to use these for selfish things, like making the other person do the dishes, or choosing what takeout to get for dinner."

I tried to give the coupon back, but Frankie shoved it into my hands.

"This is selfish. If you get laid, maybe you'll stop whining so much. I'm saving my eardrums."

He stuck his tongue out at me to show he was joking, not that I needed any reassurance. Frankie could be just as annoying as me when he wanted to be. It's why we got along so well.

"Fine." I ripped the coupon in half. "I'll do it. But when he turns me down, I'm eating all the ice cream and there's nothing you can do about it."

Frankie snorted. "You do that anyway."

Then, he handed me my phone.

I stared at the screen, hoping it would suddenly burst into flames.

Why couldn't it have broken when I

dropped it the other day?

Then I'd have an excuse not to call.

My fingers were numb as I punched in the numbers. The phone rang, and I held it up to my ear as delicately as I could.

"Hello? Who's this?"

I recognized the voice as soon as I heard it. That was definitely him. A shiver ran down my spine with a mixture of pleasure and shame that sat heavy in my belly.

"Hi. Um, this is Newton Clary. From the hospital."

"Newton?"

I held the phone away from my ear and mimed hitting my head against something.

Why had I introduced myself with my full name?

I never used my full name. It sounded so pretentious.

"Newt," I corrected myself. "We met when you came in to see the John Doe from the warehouse fire."

"I remember."

His words were sparse, with little inflection.

He remembered me, but did he remember me in a good way or a bad one?

I couldn't tell, and it made me even more nervous.

"Right, so, the DNA test came in."

A moment of silence passed. This was it. I needed to ask him out. My mouth moved, but no sound came out.

Beside me, Frankie waved me on, urging me to say something.

I could practically feel the confusion emanating from the other side of the phone.

"So, can you tell me the results?"

The way he phrased the question "can you" instead of "will you" sparked an idea in my brain. It was probably a stupid idea, but I had nothing else, so I ran with it.

"Well, unfortunately I can't divulge information like this over an open line. Medical privacy, you know. So, I need to tell you face to face. There's a coffee shop near the hospital where we could meet up. Or somewhere else, if that's not convenient for you. It doesn't even have to be a coffee shop. We can go anywhere you like."

Out of the corner of my eye, I noticed Frankie gesturing across his own throat in a clear gesture to stop. I bit my tongue against the torrent of words that wanted to spill out of me. The more nervous I was, the faster I talked. It was a bad habit I'd had since childhood and had gotten me into trouble plenty of times.

I held my breath, waiting for an answer. The silence persisted so long that for a moment I thought the line had disconnected.

Nope. Still connected. There was just no noise coming from the other side of the line. Not even the sound of breathing.

Finally, after several agonizing moments, Bastian responded. "All right. I can meet you. Name a place and I'll be there."

The moment I heard those words, part of my brain drifted off into the clouds. I gave him the address of the first coffee shop I thought of close to the hospital, and we agreed on a time and place to meet. When it was done and I hung up, I stared at Frankie in shock.

"He said yes."

Frankie hummed and rolled his head back and forth on his shoulders. "Well, technically you didn't actually ask him out. You asked him to meet you. There's a difference."

"I don't care." At this point, I was practically shouting. "He said *yes*. After everything I did, he still said yes. Oh my god, that means I'm going to have to talk to him. I... I... I can't think about this right now."

There was only so much emotional whiplash my mind could take in one day, and I had reached my limit. I needed to not think for a while.

Turning on the game console attached to the television, I picked up one of the controllers and tossed the other to Frankie. "Here. I need a second player for this new game I just got."

Frankie looked at the controller, then looked at me, then back at the controller. I could see the wheels turning in his head.

"Fine." He relented and reclined back against the couch to face the screen. "But we're not done talking about this. We need to make a plan. Date outfit. Conversation starts. Things like that."

"Plan later. Games now."

In the end, I got a few hours of reprieve to let myself recover from the excitement of the day. By the time we got back around to discussing my upcoming sort-of date with Bastian Roth, I was actually feeling more excited than nervous.

Well, no, that was a lie. I was still mostly nervous, but there was excitement as well. The good kind that made my stomach feel fluttery.

When the next day rolled around, and I opened the door to the coffee shop, my fingers couldn't stop twitching. There wasn't even any caffeine in my system yet, and I already felt over-energized. Especially, when I looked across the coffee shop and saw Bastian's familiar figure sitting in a chair on the far side of the room.

Seeing him there, I realized I'd made a mistake in my choice of coffee shop. I hadn't been thinking clearly and just picked my favorite place. *Cool Beans* had once been a comic book shop. The place almost went out of business until the owner got the idea to turn it into a coffee shop decorated with nerdy memorabilia. It even still sold comics along with coffee and pastries, and a line of vintage arcade machines stood along the back wall waiting to eat people's quarters.

It was a place where I felt comfortable, and a place where someone like Bastian

Roth absolutely did not belong. Dressed in a long black coat, flatteringly tight black t-shirt, black jeans, and fancy leather boots, he looked like the hero of a spy movie who had accidentally wandered into a kid's cartoon.

I was also really regretting my choice of outfit. Frankie had insisted that I wear the clothes I liked best. It would make me more comfortable, and there was no point in presenting a false persona. I'm a weird little nerd, and Bastian needed to be aware of that from the start.

It had sounded so logical when Frankie was explaining it, but now, looking down at myself, I felt a bit ridiculous. The orange rain jacket was already loud enough, but then I'd paired it with a lilac shirt that didn't match at all.

The worst offender, however, was my hat. It had been a gift from my grandmother for my sixth birthday. The crochet creation had been made to look like a chipmunk, with big cartoon eyes and furry little ears. It was my favorite for rainy days because the two paw-shaped flaps on the side kept my ears warm.

I'd felt comfortable when I left my apartment, but seeing Bastian sitting there waiting for me, a new wave of embarrassment left me feeling hot and cold at the same time.

Well, too late to turn back now. All I could do was charge forward.

First, however, I made a quick stop at the counter to pick up a drink and several pastries. When all else failed, I could always rely on stress eating to cheer me up.

"Hey," I greeted as I sat down in the seat across from Bastian. "Thanks, um... thanks for meeting me."

He nodded, tipping his half-finished drink at me. "I should be thanking you. You're the one bringing me the info I need."

Right. The reason we were here. This wasn't really a date. Just an exchange of information.

Caught up in the excitement of meeting with Bastian again, I hadn't actually looked at the DNA results. I pulled the file out of my bag and flipped it open on the table so we could both see the contents.

There, written right at the very top of the first page, was the answer Bastian had been waiting for.

0% match.

The John Doe lying in my hospital was not the brother of Bastian's client.

Bastian stared at the words for a moment, then took the time to leaf through the other pages before snapping the file closed.

"Well, I'm not surprised. It would have been too easy if the man we're looking for just showed up like that. Thanks again for bringing this. Now I can start looking elsewhere."

I nodded, while trying not to let my disappointment show. His words sounded like a dismissal. Now that he had what he wanted, he had no reason to stick around, and I certainly wasn't enough to keep his interest on my own.

Before he could say anything else, or I could do something shameful like begging him to stay and talk to me, an alert rang on Bastian's phone. It was a cheery little tune.

A tune I recognized.

My hand acted before my brain could speak up, and I snatched his phone off the table. There it was, right on the screen. An alert notification from one of my favorite Obscure games.

All thoughts of DNA tests and missing brothers were forgotten as I looked up at Bastian with wide eyes.

"You play *Lemur Conspiracy*?"

CHAPTER SEVEN

Sebastian

FUCK, HIS EYES were really blue. I'd noticed it before, but the lavender shirt he wore highlighted their color and made them look almost purple.

How was I supposed to respond when those eyes were looking up at me, as big as saucers, and twinkling with excitement?

My phone chimed again. Oh, right, the game. For a moment, I considered just grabbing my phone and walking out of the coffee shop. I'd never told anyone, not even my brother, that I played video games. If I did decide to tell someone about my hobby, I definitely would have picked something better than Lemur Conspiracy.

There was nothing wrong with the game. It was a fun mystery solving adventure about a lemur that escaped from a science lab, and solved mysteries using its newly acquired human intelligence and the ability to speak with animal ghosts. One of the selling points about the game was that new mysteries and clues were always being added.

Which was exactly what my phone was alerting about now. A new clue had just dropped, and the colorful cartoon art style was challenging me to come find the next piece of the mystery.

My fingers itched with a desire to start playing. I never could resist a good mystery. The rush I got from solving a difficult puzzle was almost more satisfying than anything else. It was one of the best parts about being a private investigator. There were plenty of real-life puzzles to solve.

Well, that, and the opportunity to help people.

While I hovered in indecision, Newt started scrolling through the game on my phone.

"Wow. You've solved so many of these. You even solved the Haunted Goldfish Bowl. I could never get through that one. Where'd you find the last clue?"

That had been one of my favorite levels since it was particularly difficult. Many people didn't even get past the opening. At first, it seemed like the setting for the level was a kid's bedroom. However, if the player looked inside the goldfish bowl, they would find that the little decorative house inside was actually a fully functioning mansion. The actual mystery took place inside that mansion, which was haunted by all the ghosts of the fish that had lived in that bowl before its current resident.

Blue eyes pointed toward me again, and I had no choice but to answer. "There's a safe behind the portrait in the bedroom. At the beginning of the level, when you're talking to the old lady fish, the date she mentions for their anniversary is different from what was captioned on the picture. The two numbers together are the code for the safe."

"Oh, cool." Newt put down my phone

and pulled out his own. A moment later the familiar tune for Lemur Conspiracy started playing. "A new clue just dropped. You're doing the River Maze, right?"

I looked at my phone still sitting on the table, then looked at Newt.

Was that it?

I expected snide comments about how I didn't look like the type to play video games, or maybe questions about why I was playing something meant for children. The few times in the past that I'd even hinted at liking video games, those were always the reactions I got. Newt's unquestioning acceptance caused my brain to short circuit. I stared at him dumbly, my hand hovering halfway to my phone without picking it up.

Newt must have mistaken my confusion for anger, because the light in his blue eyes dimmed. "Oh, sorry. That was rude. Can't believe I just grabbed your phone like that. I get tunnel vision when I'm excited and I forget about everything else. Even manners, apparently."

He laughed, awkwardly tugging at one of the ears on his hat. It was such a cute sight. I couldn't help but smile.

"Yeah, I'm doing the River Maze." I picked up my phone and reopened the game. I think there's a hidden room in the bottom of the boat, so hopefully, the next clue will lead us there."

Newt's smile lit up his whole face, so even his freckles seemed to glow.

"A hidden room? Really? I had no idea. No wonder I keep getting lost. I'm missing more clues than I thought."

Over the next half hour, Newt and I sat huddled around the table playing Lemur Conspiracy. We first had to double back and pick up a few clues that he had missed before we could move on to the new stuff, but I didn't mind.

One of the reasons I never told my brother about liking video games is because I didn't want to talk about it. Logically, I knew he wouldn't care and would support my interest, but he would inevitably have questions. That's how Damien showed his support for anything. By asking questions and taking an interest. It was nice, but video games were something I used to relax, and conversation took effort. So, I kept that little secret to myself.

With Newt, it was different. The other

man took over the conversation, doing most of the talking. When he asked me questions, it didn't feel like a quiz where I needed to come up with the right answer. He never asked how I felt about something, or what I preferred. He just asked me for information about the game, like where to find a clue or how to solve a puzzle. These questions were easy to answer and took no effort, which left me free to simply bask in our shared passion and excitement over the game.

I wouldn't have even minded starting the whole game over from the beginning if it meant we could keep talking a little longer.

By the end of the first half hour, we sat so close together that we were practically fused together from shoulder to hip. At some point, I'd draped one arm over the back of his chair so that we could see both phone screens at the same time. It was a completely natural action that I hadn't even thought about doing. We must have been sitting in that position for at least twenty minutes before I looked up to find his blue eyes only inches away, and I realized how close we'd drawn together.

He fit so perfectly under my arm, like he'd been designed to be just the right height for an armrest.

I smirked. "I was right."

Newt's gaze tracked the movement of my lips. "What?"

"There was a hidden room."

"Oh." He looked down again. "Yeah. The game."

Our height difference put his head under my chin, giving me a close look at his crocheted hat. So much care had been put into every detail, it was only from this distance that I could see it was handmade and not a mass-produced item.

Curious, I tugged at one of the ears.

"This is a unique design."

Newt's hands shot up to hold the sides of the hat, as if I might yank it off his head. "My grandmother made it. When I was little, she used to call me chipmunk."

The other man was obviously sensitive about it. He'd reacted so quickly as soon as the hat was touched, I wondered how often it had been stolen from him. I could picture the scene too easily. Schoolyard bullies would love to steal such a beloved item so they could taunt him with it. A boy treasuring something so cute and "unmasculine" would inevitably attract the wrong kind of attention.

I removed my hand from the hat and let my arm drape over the back of his chair again. "Chipmunk? Odd nickname. I'm sensing a story behind that."

Tension drained from Newt's shoulders when he realized I wasn't about to steal the hat or insult it. He switched off Lemur Conspiracy to instead scroll through pictures on his phone. Once he found a specific picture way back in his photo album, he held up the screen for me to see.

It showed a picture of a much younger Newt, maybe eight or nine years old. The ginger hair and freckles were the same, but his cheeks were still round with youth and his smile was slightly bucktoothed as his front teeth were visible over his bottom lip.

"It took me a while to grow into my face. Especially the teeth."

Almost as quickly as Newt brought out the picture, he immediately took it away.

"Luckily, my adult teeth grew in better proportioned, but the other kids used to tease me about it a lot. I thought I was ugly, until my grandma pointed out that round cheeks and big front teeth are the same features that chipmunks have, and they're considered cute. That must mean I'm cute as well. So, from that day on, I became her chipmunk."

The game on my phone beeped again, asking if I wanted to continue playing.

I turned off the screen and set it aside.

"She was right. You are cute."

As I'd predicted, as soon as the complement left my mouth, Newt blushed bright enough that his freckles nearly disappeared. Since he was bundled up in a rain jacket, I could only see his face. However, the small visible sliver of his neck showed that it also turned red when he blushed.

My gaze trailed downward, mapping each inch of him.

How far down did that blush go?

He was so pale, his whole body probably turned red.

My wandering eyes must have been obvious—I was really trying to hide them—because Newt suddenly started stuttering and tugging at his hat again.

"It's my favorite hat, but I shouldn't have worn it today. So stupid to wear this kind of thing on a..."

His voice suddenly died, like the word had been snatched right off his tongue, and he looked up at me with wide eyes.

I watched him for a moment, silently waiting to see if he would finish the sentence or try to correct himself. His mouth opened a few times, but no words came out.

My smirk deepened. "On a... what? Is there a reason your clothes should matter for our meeting?"

Nervously licking his lips, Newt looked down and shook his head.

I leaned a little closer, and would have been speaking directly into his ear if it wasn't covered by his hat. "Let me guess, there's not actually a rule about delivering medical information over the phone. You just wanted to meet with me." I flashed him a knowing smile.

Like a balloon that had been stuck by a pin, Newt deflated in his chair until his forehead rested on the table.

"Argh! I just... I wanted to ask you out, but I panicked and said the first excuse I could think of."

The little nurse had such over-the-top reactions, it made me want to keep teasing him, but I held back. Teasing could easily become bullying if I wasn't careful, especially since we didn't know each other that well yet.

Hopefully, if I handled this situation correctly, there would be more opportunities in the future to tease him.

I leaned back enough to give him space but didn't move my chair away. "So, is this a date?"

Without raising his head from the table, one blue eye peeked at me between orange bangs. "Maybe. If you want."

That answer wasn't as confident as I would have liked. My personality had often been labeled as "intense," and my life came with a lot of baggage. If someone was going to date me, they needed to be certain.

As I weighed my options, an idea suddenly struck me. Our conversation had been going so smoothly earlier, when we were talking about something we had equal feelings about.

Perhaps that was the key to communicating with Newt. Making sure we were equal.

I laid my head down on the table as well so that our eyes were on the same level. My height made it difficult, and my spine protested the uncomfortable arch, but the effort was worth it when surprise flashed through those beautiful blue eyes.

"I'm more concerned about what you want. But just so you know, if you had asked me out on a date when you called, I would have said yes."

Newt shot up so fast in his seat he looked like a puppet whose strings had suddenly been jerked by an inexperienced puppeteer.

"Really? You're not just saying that out of pity, right? You actually would have said yes?"

"I really would have." My spine popped when I sat up, making me feel momentarily older than my thirty-three years. "You want this to be a date, and I want this to be a date. That makes this a date." I flashed him a grin.

The joy radiating off of Newt could have turned day to night.

Who needed daylight when I had such a little ball of sunshine at my side?

He even tucked himself back under my arm, which brought a genuine smile to my face as well. The man's joy was contagious.

We talked for a little longer, discussing

other games that we liked while Newt chewed his way through the pastries he'd bought. We'd been so wrapped up in our conversation, the baked goods had sat forgotten on the table until that moment. I wondered if this was a normal example of his eating habits, and almost asked how he stayed so slim with such an appetite. However, common sense silenced my tongue. We were not close enough yet for such personal questions.

Eventually, our newly named 'date' came to an end when Newt declared that his nursing shift would be starting soon. The hospital was only a few blocks away—apparently one of the reasons Newt frequented this coffee shop—so I offered to escort him.

I worried that my offer might be taken the wrong way, like I thought he couldn't be trusted to walk on his own. Really, it was just an excuse to prolong our date. It had been so long since I'd found someone other than my brother that I could relate to, and I didn't want the interaction to end yet.

Luckily, Newt seemed to realize the true reason behind my offer and eagerly accepted. Even once we reached the hospital, he didn't try to make me leave. I entered the building with him and even followed him up the elevator to one of the higher floors. It was as though we'd reached a silent but mutual agreement to fight off our separation as much as possible.

As we wound our way through the maze of hospital hallways, we discussed our upcoming schedules to try and find a chance for another date. Next time, it would be a proper one that we both agreed to beforehand.

Eventually, we reached a door labeled "staff only" and ran out of excuses to delay the inevitable.

"I'll call you later," Newt said as he loitered just outside the door. "We need to set up a game night some time."

There were many games that required a second player that I'd never been able to play on my own. The entire multiplayer genre was now open to me and I was filled with excitement.

Yet, before I could agree to Newt's plan, I was interrupted by what amounted to a howl.

"Meehawww!"

The tortured shout came from down

the hall, and immediately put me on edge. I'd heard people cry out like that before. I'd even made such noises myself, on the night my parents were killed. The words may have been nonsense, but the tone was unmistakable.

Desperation.

Noticing my reaction, Newt brought me over to a door I'd seen before.

"Sorry. I should have warned you. The John Doe woke up. Well, sort of. He's making noise, at least. Though we still don't know what he's trying to say."

Inside the private ICU room I'd visited before, the unnamed man still lay on his bed. He looked the same. Maybe a few less bandages, but definitely not someone who would be getting up any time soon.

"Eliiiii," the man cried out, barely moving his mouth to form the word. It almost sounded like a name, but maybe that was my own active imagination trying to find meaning in noise.

"That one's new," Newt whispered to me as we stood in the doorway. "At first, it was just the one word. Mehaw? But early this morning, he started saying this second word. We're hoping it means he'll wake up soon."

Although the John Doe wasn't the man I was looking for, I still wished him a speedy recovery. I hated seeing someone in such pain, and felt guilty over the joy I'd found thanks to this unnamed man's misfortune.

After all, without the John Doe lying on that hospital bed, I wouldn't have met the fascinating little man standing beside me now.

Sadness crept into his blue eyes as Newt's gaze sank to the floor. "I hope he wakes up soon. He's held on this long. It would be a shame if he didn't recover after all this."

In a split-second decision, I took a risk and pressed a quick kiss to Newt's cheek.

"With such a dedicated nurse, of course he'll recover." I flashed him a soft, understanding smile.

Just as I'd hoped, the sadness in Newt's eyes disappeared and his face lit up with a smile once again. I decided right then and there that Newt should always be smiling. The world felt brighter when he did, and there was enough darkness in my life already.

I needed a little more light.

CHAPTER EIGHT

Sebastian

IT PROBABLY WASN'T safe to talk on the phone while driving. Thanks to my Bluetooth, I was able to keep both hands on the wheel, but Newt's voice coming through the speaker still distracted me.

"Come on," Newt begged, his words trailing off into a high-pitched whine. "Just a little hint."

I chuckled under my breath as I pictured the pout that would be on his face right that moment. "No. You said you wanted to solve it yourself."

"But I didn't think it'd be this hard. My break is almost over and I'm no closer to beating this level than I was half an hour ago," he whined.

A week had passed since our first 'date' and we'd played video games together almost every evening. We'd discovered that while I was better at puzzle solving, Newt was better at precision movements. When it came to things like platforming and speed-running, his nimble fingers somehow knew just what buttons to hit.

He absolutely crushed me at Mario Kart every time.

Of course, all of that was only online. Since our coffee shop date, we hadn't played together face-to-face again. Newt's two jobs kept him busy, so scheduling a time to meet was difficult, but I wasn't going to complain.

I had my own job as well. That was why I was driving home alone so late at night despite the rain pouring down. I needed to meet with someone who unfortunately wasn't available any other time and they'd kept me out until almost midnight.

"Okay, fine," I relented. "One hint."

Although Newt didn't say anything, I could hear him moving around as he celebrated his victory.

At first, I considered just telling him what he wanted to know, but listening to him gloat over an achievement he hadn't earned yet gave me a different idea.

"You have to breathe on yourself."

Silence rang over the line for a moment before Newt's voice exploded.

"What? That's not helpful at all. I have no idea what that means. Stop being cryptic and just *tell* me."

"You'll have plenty of time to think about it while you're working."

A beep interrupted our conversation, indicating that someone else was calling me. I recognized my brother's number immediately.

A knot of panic tightened my chest.

Why was Damien calling me?

He hated staying up late and should be in bed by now. Earlier, he'd gone out to investigate a possible lead on Jason Dahler's missing brother. The John Doe may not have been our man, but we had other leads to follow.

However, even if Damien had discovered something about Clay Dahler, there was no reason for him to call me. Anything he found could have waited until I got home.

"Newt, I need to hang up. My brother is calling. I'll talk to you later."

I almost didn't need the phone to hear him sigh. His resignation seemed to vibrate the very fabric of reality.

"Fine. I see how it is. Just hang up and leave me clueless."

My panic subsided for a moment in the wake of Newt's dramatics.

"I'll make it up to you on our date this weekend. Still on for that, right?"

"Of course. You're coming over to my place so we can play together in person. And you can meet my roommate, Frankie. You'll like him."

A distant voice could just be heard over the line. Newt exchanged a few words with the person, too far away from the phone's mic for me to hear what he said, then his voice returned.

"My break is over. I've got to go. If you want to make it up to me, then bring me one of those giant cookie-cakes."

"With M&M's instead of chocolate chips?" I asked despite already knowing the answer.

"Yep." Even though I couldn't see his smile, I could practically hear the way his mouth curved around the words. "Only a week of dating and you already know me so well. I'm not sure if that means you're too smart, or I'm too simple. Hmm. You're probably just too smart. No one's ever accused me of being simple. Bye. Talk to you later."

Then he hung up.

With the touch of a button, I switched over the Bluetooth to pick up my brother's call.

"Damien? Is something wrong?"

My brother hated talking on the phone while driving. He was paranoid about causing an accident, and never called anyone when he knew they were in a car, even if they were just a passenger. This meant that whatever he needed to tell me must be important.

"Where are you right now?"

My face stayed passive as I focused on the road, but inside I cringed. Of all the questions Damien could have demanded, it had to be one I couldn't answer.

"I'm driving right now."

I would have just left it at that, but Damien knew me too well. He'd be able to sense the omission if I wasn't more specific.

Gritting my teeth, I gripped the steering wheel tighter.

"I had a date. We went out to the movies. The theaters nearby didn't have any show times that fit with Newt's schedule, so we had to go farther away. Should be home in about half an hour."

I'd lied to my brother exactly three times in my life.

The first was when I was a kid. I hadn't yet come to terms with my sexuality and invented a fake girlfriend to prove I was straight. Damien saw right through the lie and called me out, metaphorically prying me out of the closet with a crowbar.

The second time I lied to him was right after our parents were killed. I insisted I was fine when we both knew I was having nightmares. Damien pretended to accept the lie, but he always remained nearby when I slept.

The third time I lied to him was just a few months ago, when I accepted the case I was currently working on. I knew Damien would turn down the case if asked. He'd claim it was too big for us to handle. So, I never told him about it.

Did omission still count as a lie?

Technically, I never said anything that

was untrue, but keeping secrets from him felt like lying, so it was added to the list.

Now I'd just lied to him a fourth time. It still hurt, but I must have been getting better at it because Damien accepted the lie without question.

"Right, that nurse you told me about. The one with the lizard name."

"Newts are amphibians," I automatically corrected him even as I fought the nausea building in my gut.

"Yeah, that guy. Look, I hate to ruin your night, but I need you to get home as soon as possible. I just got a weird message."

The rain started coming down harder and I turned up the windshield wipers. At night, water on the pavement made the road look like it had been encrusted with silver. It would have been beautiful, if not for the mix of guilt and dread cramping my stomach.

"Nothing is ruined. I was already on my way home. What do you mean you got a weird message?"

Damien started to say something, but I never heard him. My car suddenly lurched as it was struck from behind, causing the back wheels to spin over the wet asphalt.

"Fuck. What?"

I held tight to the wheel, struggling to get the car back under control. It swerved one way, then overcorrected and swerved the other. My heart pounded wildly in my chest, but there wasn't even time to think. My hands acted on instinct, keeping the wheel pointed in the direction I needed to go.

The car settled back in the center of the road, and I breathed for the first time in what felt like years.

For a moment, I considered pulling over to inspect the car and see what happened, but years of experience hiding from the mafia told me to keep driving. I pressed my foot down on the gas and sped up.

In my rearview mirror, I caught a glimpse of a car driving close behind me. I would have assumed they lost control in the rain and accidentally hit me, except their headlights were dark and they were tailing me too close to be an accident.

Whoever was sitting behind the wheel of the other car had hit me on purpose.

The other car—a black sedan that was almost invisible in the dark—lunged for my back bumper again.

"Fucking hell," I shouted as I swerved, just barely avoiding another collision.

In the back of my mind, I realized I could hear Damien's voice shouting at me through the still connected Bluetooth, but there was no time to answer him.

The black car sped up until it was right beside me, close enough for our wing mirrors to scrape against each other. Blackout windows blocked my view inside. The car may as well have been a ghost, emerging out of the darkness and driven by no one.

I slammed on the breaks, nearly hydroplaning on the wet road. The black car was taken by surprise and didn't stop as quickly. I turned the wheel and sped off down a side street, trying to put as much distance between me and my pursuer as possible.

The black car followed, always just a few feet behind.

"Sebastian. What the hell is going on?"

My brother's angry yelling finally registered in my brain, as he shouted frantically at me through the speaker.

"Someone just tried to run me off the road."

The black car was gaining. I pressed the accelerator all the way to the floor, but my car was old and was already pushing its top speed. It couldn't go any faster.

There was less traffic at night, but Baton Rouge was a big city. Its streets were never empty. I swerved around a tan station wagon without slowing down. My rear bumper nearly clipped them. I flinched but kept my hands on the wheel.

Damien was still shouting, loud enough to drown out the thundering rain.

"What do you mean someone tried to run you off the road? What're you doing? Get out of there."

"I'm trying." I grit my teeth as I swerved around another car, cutting into the oncoming lane to avoid a collision. "They're following me. I can't get rid of them."

"Hold on. I'm calling the police. Where are you?"

"I'm just outside of... shit."

Out of the corner of my eye, I saw another dark vehicle appear beside me, headlights off and windows blacked out just like the first one. It seemed to come out of nowhere, boxing me in on one side while the first car continued to pursue me from behind.

I wasn't driving anywhere specific. Wasn't even paying attention to the road signs. My only instinct was to flee.

Then I noticed a bridge up ahead.

It shouldn't have taken me by surprise. Baton Rouge sat beside the Mississippi River, so there were plenty of lakes and rivers dotting the area. It was impossible to get anywhere without crossing a bridge at some point.

The bridge was relatively small, and the road merged so there was only one lane going in each direction. The car beside me knocked against my side while at the same time the first car slammed into me from behind. My car lurched to the side and bounced off the guardrail protecting the edge of the bridge.

A stabbing pain shot through my neck as my head whipped back and bounced against my seat. One of my hands slipped off the steering wheel. I desperately grabbed for it, trying to regain control, but it was too late.

One of the black cars slammed into me again. The door beside me bent inward with a screech of buckling metal. My car hit the guardrail again, breaking through the protective barrier.

For a moment, I felt weightless. My car hung in mid-air with me inside.

Then I hit the water with a shattering impact.

The river was too shallow to support the weight of my car. It slammed down nose first, crashing right into the bottom of the riverbed.

Pain erupted everywhere. I hung limply in my seatbelt, barely able to breathe through the shock.

The car stood on its front end for a moment, so I faced directly into the ground. The engine and hood had completely crumpled like it was mere tinfoil instead of steel.

As if in slow motion, the current of the river pushed against the car, tipping it to the side. It moved slowly at first, then all at once it toppled sideways.

The second smaller impact sent numbness spreading through my limbs, and my ears buzzed like a broken television. I may have blacked out for a moment, it was hard to tell, but I was brought back by the feeling of something cold running down my leg.

SEBASTIAN

Water was leaking into the car and gradually filling the interior.

The car had landed on the driver's side, so my door pressed directly into the riverbed. The water wasn't deep, but it would be enough to drown me if I stayed trapped inside the twisted box of metal.

I needed to get out.

I blindly fumbled for the latch of my seatbelt one-handed. I don't remember finding it, but I must have, for a moment later I tried to climb up to the passenger's seat that hovered above me.

Pain, like fire burning my skin, raced up my right leg. Between the repeated blows from the other cars, then smashing into the ground, the front portion of my car had collapsed around my legs. My left leg was mostly fine, but pieces of jagged metal pierced through my right leg like the teeth of a monster.

Water continued to flow into the car. I needed to escape through the passenger door, but I was pinned.

"Fuck."

With shaking hands, I tugged at the metal piercing my flesh. All I did was smear blood around. The metal wouldn't budge.

"Goddamn it."

Adrenaline pumped through my veins, turning my vision red at the edges.

Or maybe that was blood leaking into my eyes. I definitely had several other injuries, but my leg was the biggest concern.

I needed something stronger than human hands to pry the metal jaws free.

My coat.

I always wore the same long black coat whenever the weather permitted. It was my favorite piece of clothing. Not only did it have a lot of pockets, but there were also bulletproof panels sewn into strategic places along the front.

My bloody fingers tore at the coat's inner lining to produce a piece of Kevlar about five inches long. I wedged the Kevlar panel between my flesh and the broken metal, using it like a lever to bend the metal away from my leg. There wasn't enough time to completely free myself. The water inside the car was already a foot deep.

I focused on the biggest pieces trapping me. Once those were out of the way, I took a deep breath and yanked my leg free.

I screamed. For a moment, I feared I'd torn my leg completely off. Yet, when I looked down it was still attached to my body. Broken and bleeding, but still there.

Thank fuck.

Using my arms and my uninjured leg, I pulled myself across the seats to the passenger door. That side of the car pointed up to the sky. I could see stars through the window.

It had stopped raining.

I yanked at the handle and shoved at the door with my shoulder until it opened. Dragging my broken leg behind me, I slid out the door on my belly and fell into the river.

Water rushed into my mouth and nose. I thrashed my arms in a poor imitation of swimming. Everything felt bitingly cold, except my leg, which burned white hot.

I couldn't even tell which way the riverbank was. Pushing back the pain and fear, I just picked a direction and started moving. The water was shallow enough that I could push my good leg against the bottom of the riverbed, helping to propel me forward through the current.

It may have been hours, or maybe just

minutes, but eventually, I grabbed onto something solid. I dragged myself up onto the riverbed and collapsed into the mud, gasping, my chest heaving with each strangled, painful breath.

My vision faded in and out. No matter how desperately I tried to stay awake, my strength had run dry. My brain was shutting down whether I liked it or not.

Just before everything went black, a thought drifted through my mind.

Maybe this was my punishment for lying to my brother.

CHAPTER NINE

Newt

MY SHIFT AT the hospital was only halfway over, but it already felt like it had lasted a week. I'd spent the entire first half of my break looking forward to calling Bastian on my break, only for the infuriating man to leave me with an incomprehensible clue for the video game level I couldn't beat.

An hour later and it was still bouncing around my head.

"You have to breathe on yourself," I grumbled as I sat at the front desk filing paperwork. "What does that even mean? Stupid Bastian. He's lucky he's hot, or I wouldn't forgive him."

Although my words sounded angry, anyone passing by would have known I didn't mean them due to the smile on my face.

I was dating someone.

I still couldn't believe it.

We'd talked every day this week, and so far, Bastian had taken every moment of weirdness I'd thrown at him in stride. At first glance, I hadn't expected him to be so accepting. He seemed like the kind of guy who took life seriously. His sharp, dark eyes surveyed the world around him like he was judging whether it was worth his attention or not.

Yet, under his all black wardrobe and broad shoulders, I found a man with a relaxed sense of humor and a surprising preference for wholesome entertainment.

Maybe it was too soon to think such things after only a week, but I could see us becoming serious. I'd never had a proper boyfriend before. The few flings I'd had in college didn't count.

Sucking off a drunk frat boy in the bathroom during a party couldn't compare to even a single moment just sitting around talking with Bastian.

Although now that my mind had wandered onto the topic, I couldn't help picturing what sex with Bastian would be like.

Would he be strong and domineering?

Soft and considerate?

Confident?

Shy?

Any one of those would be fine with me. I didn't have many preferences in bed, but I was eager to find out if we were compatible.

I realized I'd been sitting behind the desk daydreaming for a while. The papers in front of me were the same ones I'd looked at ten minutes ago. At this rate, I wasn't going to get any work done.

Sick leave was a thing. Every employee got a certain number of days they could call off for the sake of their health.

Was it possible to also get off work for being too horny?

"Sorry, boss, I can't cover my shift today. I'm too busy fantasizing about the hot guy I'm dating."

"What was that?"

I jumped, not realizing anyone was behind me. One of the regular nurses stood there, clipboard braced on her hip in a way that made her look busy. I knew that stance. I used it all the time when I had nothing to do but didn't want to get pulled into anyone else's work.

"Oh, uh, nothing. Just talking to myself. Do you need anything?"

"Nope. Slow night, so far. Though, I think we have a car crash victim coming in."

I reshuffled my paperwork to give my hands something to do and hide how unproductive I'd been.

"Hopefully, it's nothing too serious."

She shrugged and moved the clipboard to her other hip so she could check something on the computer. "The message we received says that they drove off a bridge. Probably drunk. The ambulance should be here in about two minutes."

"Okay, I'll prepare for a new arrival." I scanned the waiting room for any patients that might cause problems. There was an older woman with an ingrown toenail, and a man with a minor burn on his arm. Nothing that couldn't wait until after we'd dealt with the car crash victim.

Just as I stood from the desk with a stack of papers in hand, the paramedics arrived with our new patent. Since I also worked as a paramedic, I recognized several of the people pushing their way through the door. That was nothing new, and I didn't even blink at the sight of familiar faces.

Then I looked at the patient on the gurney and found a familiar face there as well. The papers fell from my hand, scattering all over the floor.

"Bastian."

In a daze, I watched the gurney pass by and disappear through another door.

No, it couldn't be.

My eyes must be wrong.

My feet carried me after the gurney, kicking aside papers with each step. Someone called my name—the other nurse, maybe—but I paid them no mind.

Following the gurney brought me to a room with an open door where a doctor and several nurses were already working. I wanted to help, or at least move close enough to get a better look at the figure lying on the bed, but my feet were rooted to the floor.

"Nurse Clary. What are you doing? That paperwork needed to be filed an hour ago. Get back to work. This isn't your patient.”

Still lost in a stunned fog, I looked over at Administrator Constella who stood next to me tapping her foot.

“I know him. At least, I think I do.”

Administrator Constella demanded further clarification, but a hole had appeared in the bustle of activity inside the room. I took the opportunity to stumble over to the patient's bedside, praying that my initial observation had been wrong.

It was the only time I could remember hating being right.

Bastian lay on the bed, bare from the chest up and covered in cuts and bruises. The worst were the cut on his forehead that matted his hair with blood and the dark bruising along his ribs that indicated they were probably broken.

“Bastian.” The name felt wrong on my lips. As if, by naming him, I'd made Bastian's tragedy real.

I trailed my hand lightly over his chest and down his stomach to stop at the top of the sheet covering him. Something didn't look right. The outline of his legs under the sheet was the wrong shape.

Terrified of what I'd find, I lifted the

sheet. More cuts and bruises marred his left leg, but it was his right one that caught my attention. The paramedics had done what they could to stabilize the limb, but I could still see deep gashes in his flesh, some all the way down to the bone. The leg also sat at an odd angle, meaning it was broken in at least one place.

Overall, it was an ugly wound that was going to take a long time to heal. Even then, scars would still be left behind.

Administrator Constella grabbed my wrist and pulled me away. "What are you doing? You know better."

"I know him," I replied. "He's my... we're dating."

"Yes, I heard you the first time. That's exactly why you can't be here."

I stared at her blankly as she dragged me out of the room.

"Huh?"

She sighed, but her usual stern expression lacked its typical edge.

"Conflict of interest. Nurses and doctors cannot work with patients that they know. You need to step away and let others take care of this."

I hated that idea.

How could I just leave Bastian lying

there in the hands of strangers?

However, I wasn't feeling very confident at the moment. My hands trembled even after Administrator Constella let them go. It was probably for the best that I didn't get involved with Bastian's care. In my current state, I'd probably just mess up and hurt him more.

Administrator Constella dropped me back off at the front desk, where I focused on picking up the papers I dropped. Hunting down each and every one turned out to be an arduous task, as many had used the opportunity to take flight and ended up several rooms away. One page had even somehow managed to slip under the door of the women's restroom. That one took me nearly ten minutes to find.

Half an hour after Bastian's arrival, I was once again sitting behind the front desk, filing paperwork, just as I had been doing earlier. I didn't feel any calmer, but I was at least able to think straight again.

No one had shown up for Bastian. That didn't strike me as odd, at first. Normal citizens couldn't drive as fast as an ambulance, so it took them time to get to the hospital. But surely half an hour should have been long enough for someone to show up. Bastian hadn't mentioned many family members, but I knew he had a brother.

What was the man's name?

It was short and started with a 'D'.

Dan?

No, too ordinary.

Dell?

No, definitely not. I'd remember if Bastian's brother was named after a computer.

Daz?

Yes, that was it. I remembered asking Bastian if Daz was actually a name, or if it was short for something. Apparently, it was a name. The brothers must have had interesting parents to choose such an unusual name for their first son, but the one time I asked about Bastian's parents, he got so quiet that I never dared ask again.

Bastian claimed he and his brother were close. Surely at least Daz should be here to support Bastian through his injuries.

Unless Daz didn't know.

Quickly turning toward the computer, I looked up Bastian's file. He was listed as unnamed. Whatever had happened to

Bastian, no one knew who he was, which meant no one had contacted anyone for him.

I didn't have Daz's number, but I did have the number for Alias Investigations, the PI firm that Bastian ran with his brother. Hopefully, Daz would pick up, because I didn't know how else to get a hold of him, and it would be hours before I could leave work to visit in person.

The phone hadn't even finished ringing once before it was picked up.

"Bastian? What the hell? Where are you?"

"Um, Daz Roth?"

A moment of silence passed where I could hear the man on the other end of the line breathing heavily. "Yes. Who is this?"

"I'm Newt Clary." It occurred to me that Bastian may not have told Daz about me. I didn't even know if Bastian was out to his family. Getting a call in the middle of the night from a hospital would be a traumatic way for the man to find out about his brother's sexuality.

Luckily, Daz put my fears to rest with his next sentence.

"You're the guy Bastian's been seeing.

Is he with you?"

"Well, sort of. He's at the hospital where I work. As a patient. Apparently, there was a car accident. The doctors are working on him now, but he was still unconscious when I saw him."

I could hear shuffling on the other end of the line and the shattering sound of something breaking. Daz cursed and his voice disappeared for a moment. When he returned, he was panting. "What hospital are you at? I'm coming right now."

I told him the name of the hospital and rapidly listed off the address. As soon as I finished speaking, I was met with the sound of a dead line. Staring at the phone for a moment in confusion, I realized he must have hung up. The man had been in such a rush to leave, hopefully he'd heard the address before he hung up or else he might end up at the wrong hospital.

Less than ten minutes later, a man who had to be Daz Roth came running through the door. He looked a lot like Bastian, equally tall and broad with the same intensely dark eyes. The only difference was that Daz's hair lacked the little wave at the front that caused Bastian's bangs to fall across his forehead. Instead, Daz had a short beard that highlighted the cut of his jaw.

I didn't get a chance to speak with the man. Now wasn't the time. As soon as he reached the front desk, he locked eyes with me, like he already recognized me and knew I would give him what he wanted.

I told him Bastian's room number and pointed him in the right direction.

With a nod of thanks, Daz took off down the hall, slowing down just enough to technically be walking instead of running.

I breathed half a sigh of relief. Not a full sigh. Bastian was still injured, but at least there was someone with him now.

The rest of my shift passed by in a blur. Thinking back on it later, I wouldn't even remember the next few hours. It was like I blinked, and suddenly, I was off the clock and standing outside Bastian's room.

The elation I felt when I saw that Bastian was awake could have sent me floating above the clouds. If I could bottle that emotion and store it for later, I would never need to walk again.

Next to Bastian's bed, Daz sat in a

chair, bent forward with his elbows on his knees. The man looked tired. They both did, but Bastian was obviously more physically tired while Daz seemed to be suffering from emotional exhaustion.

"We'll talk about this more later," I heard Daz say as I approached.

Bastian's response was uncharacteristically subdued. "D, I'm sorry. I—"

Daz held up a hand to silence him. "No. We'll talk about it later. You lied to me. I didn't know where you were. But... that's not important right now. You need to focus on getting better, and I need to find out who attacked you."

Bastian was too busy looking at his brother to notice me standing in the doorway. It was Daz who saw me first and waved for me to come in.

"Your car has a dashcam. If it can be salvaged, maybe the video will show us something helpful about the other cars. It's a place to start, at least."

Daz turned to leave, but Bastian caught his sleeve. "Let me know what you find out. I want to help."

With the patience of an overworked mother, Daz sighed and pulled Bastian's hand off him before tucking the sheets tighter around his brother.

"The only thing you should be worried about is healing. I'll take care of this." It looked like Bastian was going to argue, but Daz pointed a scolding finger at him. "No. I don't want to hear it. You're on time-out right now. Stay put, and don't go poking your nose into things. It looks like your boyfriend is here to keep you company. Just focus on that, and we'll talk more later."

After saying his piece, Daz left. As we passed each other in the doorway, he patted my shoulder. Although he didn't say anything, that one little gesture felt like acceptance.

With no other people to stand in my way, and Bastian's attention now focused on me, I ran to his bedside.

"Oh my god. What happened? We were just talking on the phone, and then... then you showed up at the hospital like this. They said you were in a car accident."

I sat on the edge of the bed, careful not to jostle him or touch him in any way. Based on the notes I read, I knew they had him hooked up to painkillers, but I still didn't want to risk causing him any more harm.

Bastian grabbed my hand and interlaced our fingers. "It wasn't an accident. Someone ran me off the road on purpose."

What followed was a short but horrifying story about a high-speed chase in the rain that ended with Bastian crashing into the river. I practically stopped breathing until Bastian finally concluded the story by describing how he managed to climb onto the riverbank before passing out.

If it had been me in such a situation, I would have died. There was no question about that. I admired his tenacity and his fight to survive, but at that moment all I wanted to do was throw my arms around the man and make sure nothing bad ever happened to him again.

"So, someone really tried to kill you. Have you contacted the police? Do they have any idea who it is? Oh, is this because you're a private investigator? Does it have something to do with one of your cases?"

Bastian tipped his head to the side in thought, then flinched. I'd read in his notes that he had whiplash on top of everything else. Every movement he made was going to hurt for a while.

Still holding onto me with one hand, he used the other to rub the back of his neck. "It might be related to one of our cases, but... there is another possibility." He hesitated, obviously debating with himself over what he was about to say.

I waited in silence for him to come to a decision. We had all the time in the world. I wasn't going anywhere.

"What do you know about the Italian mafia?"

Such an out of the blue question caused my brain to stop working for a moment as I struggled to comprehend what I was being asked.

"Not much. I mean, I've seen the Godfather a few times, but that's probably not accurate."

Bastian shrugged, and even that small movement made him wince against the pain. "I wouldn't know. I could never bring myself to watch the movie. It... it hit too close to home. I need you to understand a few things. Some of which may come as a shock but no matter what you need to keep this information to yourself for our safety. When I was eighteen and Daz was twenty—his real name is actually Damien—our parents were killed by the mafia."

Of all the things I expected to hear, a connection to the mafia was not something I was prepared for. My noncommittal "Oh," probably didn't inspire a lot of confidence, but Bastian kept talking anyway. It was like, once he started explaining, he couldn't stop until he reached the end.

"I don't know what our parents did to get the mafia's attention. If they were innocent, or if they were mixed up in something they shouldn't have been. Whatever the reason, it must have been important for the Mafia Boss, a man named David Russo, to personally kill them himself. My brother and I saw it happen. We were determined to testify against that monster and make him pay for what he did to our parents. It worked. He went to jail, though not for as long as I would have liked. However, as soon as we testified in court, my brother and I became marked men. Russo's men came after us, so we had to go into witness protection."

"At least you had some protection. So that's good, right?" I tried to sound as positive as possible, but Bastian was already shaking his head.

"No. Russo must have had people inside the FBI. He found out where we were and his goons tried to kill us again. Almost succeeded that time. My brother and I went on the run. We hid from both the mafia and the FBI after that. It worked. We stayed alive, and eventually, it seemed like everyone forgot about us. We've managed to live peacefully for years now, but..." He trailed off, lost in memories I could only guess at.

However, I didn't need to guess the end of the story. That was as obvious as the stitches on Bastian's forehead. "Now you're worried that this David Russo Mafia Boss dude has found you again."

Bastian didn't even try to deny it. He just immediately agreed while looking down at our clasped hands. "I know this is a lot, especially after only knowing each other for a week. You didn't sign up for all this. Maybe it's better if we—"

I cut him off before he could finish that thought. "If you're about to break up with me out of some heroic need to protect me, don't. Get that thought out of your head right now." I shook my hand free from his grip, but rather than leave, I leaned closer to hug him as gently as I could.

"I know I don't seem like the strongest person. I'm weird and I'm small. I have no experience with the kind of hardships that you've described. In fact, compared to what you've been through, my life has been pretty easy up until now. However, I'm not such a coward that I would run away from someone who's in danger. People tried to kill you tonight. That's not a reason to leave you. That's a reason to protect you."

When I felt Bastian's arms wrap around my waist to embrace me, I couldn't help myself. I caught his mouth in a kiss. I meant for it to be a chaste gesture, but it ended up being much more passionate than intended.

Bastian must have been about to speak when I kissed him, because his mouth was slightly open. My tongue automatically slipped between his lips. Bastian gasped, startled at first.

I could understand the reaction. I'd startled myself as well, but I didn't back down. My mouth stayed locked with his, and after a moment, he relaxed into the kiss. His hand even cradled the back of my head and pulled me closer.

I would have preferred our first proper kiss to be when we were both whole and healthy, but a kiss was still a kiss. Just as I'd expected, Bastian was an excellent kisser. He was gentle, yet demanding as he tipped my head to the side so he could devour me properly. I felt the thrill of it all the way down to my toes and moaned against his mouth.

When we needed to breathe, we parted as little as possible so that our lips continued to brush. Then, once we'd caught our breath, we came together again, even more desperate than before.

There was no telling how long the kiss lasted. The only thing that mattered was that Bastian was here, in my arms, and not dead at the bottom of a river somewhere.

Eventually, we reached a point where we either had to stop, or risk getting kicked out of the hospital for indecent exposure. We pulled apart and I sat up straight. Most of my hair had broken free from its ponytail to hang messily around my face. It didn't even really count as a ponytail, just a tuft of hair at the back of my head. Frankie called it my rabbit tail, and I had to admit the description fit.

One day I would have to either cut it or commit to growing it long.

Still breathing heavily, I finger-combed my hair back into some semblance of order, though there was nothing I could do about my swollen lips or the blush staining my face. Anyone who looked at me would instantly know I'd just been kissed within an inch of my life.

I tried to speak, but my voice came out in an embarrassing squeak. Clearing my throat, I tried again with slightly better results.

"I don't have a lot to offer. I can't fight off the bad guys for you. But I am a nurse, and you're injured. Those two things go hand in hand. So, while I may not be able to protect you, I can at least help you with your wounds."

For the first time since arriving at the hospital, Bastian smiled. "Oh, really. You're going to be my personal nurse? I'm honored."

"You better be honored. I don't offer this kind of service to just anyone." I propped myself up against the pillow next to him and leaned my head on his shoulder, one of the few places I knew he wasn't injured. "Just so you know, Mr. Roth, I don't play nurse for free. I expect compensation. Preferably in the form of more kisses."

My head jostled when he laughed. He tried to hide his gasp as the movement aggravated his injuries, but I still heard.

We both silently agreed not to mention how much pain he was obviously in and continued our charade that everything was fine.

"More kisses?" he said when his painful laughter died down. "I can do that. Though, I might have something better."

"Better? What could possibly be better?"

He smirked at me, and for a moment he looked just as carefree as our first date. "Mirrors."

The baffled look I gave him nearly sent him into another laughing fit.

"Ha, ha. Ow. Ha. Stop looking at me like that. It's too cute. I can't handle it right now."

"I think I need to call the doctor. You might be concussed, because you're talking nonsense, Bastian.”

With one hand he tipped my chin up. I thought he was going to kiss me again, but instead he just let our foreheads rest against each other.

“Sebastian. My real name is actually Sebastian. It’s not nonsense. That clue I gave you about the level you can’t beat. The answer is mirrors. You have to inspect each mirror in the level. One of them has a secret message written on it that you’ll reveal by breathing on the glass.” He flashed me a cocky grin.

“Oh. Sebastian. I like that. Thank you for sharing that with me. Hmm, breathe on yourself,” I repeated his earlier clue. “I see now. You think you’re so clever. Don’t you, *Sebastian*?” I flashed him a smile, his name on my tongue feeling right somehow.

“Well, one of us is lying injured in a hospital bed, and one of us isn’t. So, I’m clearly not that clever.”

From that point on, the conversation remained casual. We had some very serious discussions waiting for us in our future, but now was not the time for that. Now was the time for relaxing, enjoying each other’s company, and being grateful that we were both alive.

And I was. No one could say I wasn't grateful that Sebastian had survived.

Yet, a part of me wished that we could turn back the clock to just a few hours ago, when beating a level in a video game was the only thing we had to worry about.

CHAPTER TEN

Sebastian

I COULD WALK just fine. Damien and Newt didn't need to hover around me like fruit flies looking for their next snack.

So what if I tripped twice walking from the car into my apartment. I was still getting used to the crutches that the hospital had saddled me with. Surely a learning curve was to be expected.

"Bas, slow down," Damien scolded me when my crutches accidentally banged against the front door.

Why had I chosen to live in an apartment above our office in a building with no elevator?

The stairs hadn't seemed like a big deal when we'd purchased the place, but now they were proving to be a real hindrance.

Damien tried to grab me under the arm to support me, but I knocked my other crutch against his shin.

"I'm fine."

With an exasperated sigh, Damien looked toward Newt while gesturing at me. "Reason with him. Maybe he'll listen to you."

Their shared concern for me had created an instant camaraderie between my brother and Newt. I would have been glad to see them getting along if they weren't using it to gang up on me.

Newt's shorter height allowed him to slip under my arm and drape it over his shoulder. "Come on. Let's get you inside so you can sit down. You've already been walking too long."

I didn't dare fend him off the same way I did with my brother. Damien and I sparred regularly, so I knew he could take a hit. Newt, on the other hand, likely bruised easily and I'd feel terrible if he got injured just from trying to help me.

Giving in, I let them guide me through

the door.

Newt paused for a moment at the sight of my apartment. It wasn't a typical set up. Most of the lounging space had been dedicated to workout equipment and a sparring mat. A single couch, chair, and television had been squished into what was supposed to be the dining area. However, Newt didn't say anything about the unique decor choices, and helped me navigate to the couch without tripping over the dumbbells lying on the floor.

When I finally sat down, I refused to sigh in relief. My brother and Newt would only use it as evidence that they were right, and I needed to take things easier.

As my pain meds wore off, everything hurt a lot more than before. The result of my car "accident" left me with a wide variety of injuries. The stitches holding together the cut on my forehead itched like crazy and my bruised ribs hurt if I inhaled too deeply.

My right leg, however, was the worst. Multiple bones were broken, and even my femur was cracked, which the doctors informed me was a difficult bone to injure. Not to mention the deep tissue damage from where the car's metal had cut into my leg.

All in all, my right leg was going to take a while to heal. Even I could tell that much, but that didn't mean Damien and Newt needed to treat me like an invalid. Thanks to the aid of a cast and crutches, I could still stand on my own.

"I'm fine," I tried to insist when Newt propped my injured leg up on a stool with a pillow underneath.

He looked down at me from where he stood, hands on hips and a square set to his shoulders. "You are not fine, Sebastian Roth. The doctors almost operated on your leg to pin the bone in place. The only reason they didn't is because the tibia and fibula broke cleanly, and the crack in your femur was deemed minor enough to heal on its own. But that could change if you keep moving around and exacerbate it. You're already looking at a long recovery time. If they do end up having to operate on it, then it'll be even longer."

Perhaps it was inappropriate for the situation, but watching Newt take control of the situation was kind of hot. My babbling little chipmunk became an indomitable mama bear when it came to other people's well being.

Heaving a deep sigh just to make my displeasure known, I relaxed back against the couch. "Fine. Do what you want."

Once he got his way, Newt immediately returned to his typical self and began fluffing the pillows around me.

Sitting in the chair across from the couch, Damien raised an eyebrow. He didn't say anything, but he didn't need to. I knew him well enough to interpret his slightest facial expression.

That eyebrow was both asking how the fuck Newt knew my real name, and making fun of me for giving in so quickly.

I glared at him. "Shut up."

He shrugged. "I didn't say anything. I'm just glad to see you taking care of yourself."

The levity was appreciated, but it didn't last long. Damien's teasing expression melted away and was replaced with a serious scowl.

"All right, *Sebastian*, you need to talk to me." Damien put a slight sarcastic emphasis on my name, pushing the point even more.

I shrugged in response. I refused to explain why I felt the need to be honest with Newt about that. Damien of all people should understand, seeing as how he'd recently found the men of his dreams and he hadn't lied to them about his name at all. It was a thing. Honesty. I didn't want to start my possible relationship with the copper-haired cutie with a pack of lies. So be it.

"Brother, I waited while you were in the hospital, but now you need to tell me what the fuck is going on. You weren't out with Newt the night you were attacked. So where were you and why the fuck did you lie to me about it?"

I knew that question was coming. Yet, once the words were put into the air, I didn't know what to say. My gaze instinctively drifted toward Newt, who sat at my side.

He stood from the couch. "I can step out if you need some privacy. This has to do with your PI cases, right?"

Before he could leave, I tugged his arm to guide him back to my side. "Technically, it's not an official case since I volunteered and didn't accept any money. But first, I want to apologize for using you in my lie. That wasn't fair. I just couldn't think of anything else that

Damien would believe."

Newt's fingers interlaced with mine. "I forgive you, but only if you tell your brother the truth now." He gave me a face that I assumed was supposed to look like a scowl, but it looked rather adorable instead.

"All right." I sighed.

Keeping our fingers locked together, I ran my free hand through my hair and flinched when it snagged. I really needed a shower after spending several days in the hospital. "I'll explain. Damien, could you get a file from my bedroom? It's in the bottom drawer of the nightstand by the window."

My brother smirked. "You mean the one where you keep your porn magazines?"

Since I was currently lying on all the pillows, I couldn't throw one at him, so I made do with flipping him my middle finger.

He laughed then stood to do as I asked.

I grumbled under my breath, pretending to be annoyed when really, I was relieved. If Damien was still willing to tease me, then he wasn't too mad. I would hate for this incident to ruin my relationship with my brother.

Newt was staring at me. I could feel the weight of his gaze running over my skin.

I looked over to find him giving me a perplexing look.

"What?"

His eyebrow raised in a chilling imitation of my brother. "Porn magazines? Really?"

Internally, I cursed my brother with every creative insult I knew. Although he was in another room, I swore I could hear him laughing.

"I use them to hide things. It discourages people from snooping when they open a drawer and that's the first thing they see."

Newt had come to pick me up from the hospital right after his paramedic shift, so he was still wearing his uniform. The navy-blue shirt and high-vis jacket created an odd clash of colors but couldn't detract from his delighted smile.

"Oh, no, I don't care about your masturbation material. But, magazines? Really? When the Internet exists? How old school are you?"

I would have normally responded to

his teasing with a clever comeback of my own, but I was too tired. So, I pinched his side instead.

"Brat. I thought you were mad."

Newt squirmed and swatted at my hand. "What would I be mad about? That you have a sex drive? I certainly hope so."

Although he tried to be subtle, there was no missing the way his eyes flicked up and down my body. I knew I didn't present a very impressive sight at that moment, bruised and broken, and severely in need of a shower. I was anything but sexy.

Still, if Newt could find me desirable even like this, then I probably didn't have to worry about our bedroom compatibility.

Now, if only I could capitalize on that. We hadn't slept together yet, but I'd been hoping our next date would provide an opportunity. That plan went out the window the moment my car went off the road.

Before I could voice any of that, Damien returned with the file. Plans for my future sex life would have to wait as I once again focused on business.

I spread out the contents of the file over the floor since there was no table near the couch. It mostly consisted of birth certificates and a few pictures. Not nearly as much information as I wish I had.

"I keep an eye on certain Internet forums where people ask for help, just in case there's anything interesting. A woman is looking for her daughter, so I reached out to her."

I pulled out a record of our private messages to prove I was telling the truth and handed it to Damien.

"Her name is Layla Thomas. She was seventeen when she got pregnant and decided to give the baby up for adoption. A few years later, she wanted to check up on the girl and see how she was doing. It was a closed adoption, so she had no way of finding the kid, and every appeal she made to the courts was ignored, so she hired a private investigator. The person she hired discovered that there was no record of the adoption. In fact, there was no record of her daughter ever being born."

This time, I handed Damien the largest stack of papers in the file containing birth records of every child born in the state of Louisiana on the correct date. Layla

Thomas and her daughter were nowhere to be found on that list.

"After discovering that, the investigator suddenly dropped her case with no explanation, and she couldn't get anyone else to take the case, either. I had a feeling something was going on, so I volunteered to look into it."

Damien sighed as he leafed through the pages. "Of course you did. There are kids involved. So, what have you found so far?"

I shifted in my seat and flinched when the movement jostled my leg. "At least a dozen similar cases of children put up for adoption who just disappeared from the system. So far, I've only been focusing on Louisiana, but for all I know this could be happening all across the country."

The paper slapped against the floorboards when Damien threw them down. "Why didn't you take this info to the authorities, or Mason, or at least come to me?"

"Because I didn't have any solid proof. It would be easy to write this off as a clinical error and forge a few documents to cover it up. I needed something more substantial. The night I was attacked, I went to meet the administrator for a hospital where multiple children had disappeared. They claimed to have information for me, and that was the only time they could meet. But they never showed up. After everything, all I've got is a few missing records."

I could practically see the wheels turning in Damien's head as he studied the contents of the file. We'd worked together for so long that I was certain he saw what I saw.

"If kids are going missing on this large of a scale, then it must be an organized group." He sorted through the pages again, slower this time. "There aren't a lot of reasons to kidnap this many kids except..."

He trailed off, obviously uncomfortable, so I finished the thought for him.

"Except for sex trafficking."

Damien nodded, one hand stroking over his beard. "But the real question is, why attack you now? The meeting with the administrator was obviously a trap to lure you out, but why? Killing someone is a drastic measure. You must have gotten closer to the truth than you realized, and it scared them."

He scooped up the papers and stuffed them back in the file. "I'm going to go over this and see what I can uncover. Then I'm going to send a copy over to Mason. Some of the FPA's contacts might have more information. Is this everything you have?"

"You've got three months of work in your hands. There's also a jump-drive taped to the inside of the file. That holds a digitized record of everything I've uncovered so far."

"All right. Perfect. That saves me transcribing it all for Mason." He tucked the file under his arm then pointed a finger at me. "You should not have been working on this alone, Brother. You know that."

I ducked my head, knowing he was right. I just hadn't wanted to go to anyone with it until I knew I was right.

Damien carded his fingers through his hair and sighed. "I'll be downstairs in the office getting started with this. From now on, the only thing you're doing is recovering. Newt, make sure he stays here and actually rests."

Newt saluted like a soldier accepting marching orders. "Yes, sir!"

I sighed. With the two of them working

together, I'd never get away with anything ever again.

After giving me one last pointed look, Damien headed for the office.

The door to the apartment closed behind him, leaving Newt and I alone. I leaned my head back against the couch, letting the exhaustion of the last few days pull my eyelids closed. Beside me, I felt Newt get up, but I didn't bother to look at what he was doing. Everything confidential concerning our cases was kept in the office downstairs, so he couldn't get into any trouble.

A few minutes later, Newt tapped me on the shoulder and held out a mug in front of my face. Just from the aroma, I could tell it was filled with my favorite tea. I took the mug, wrapping my fingers around its warmth.

"Thanks. How'd you know Oolong was my favorite?"

Newt rocked back on his heels with his hands clasped behind his back. "There were only two kinds of tea in your kitchen. I noticed Damien drinking Earl Gray in the hospital cafeteria, so I figured the Oolong had to be yours."

There wasn't enough sugar, but I

drank the tea eagerly. Everything at the hospital tasted the same. I asked for coffee once and the drink I got was somehow burnt and under-brewed at the same time.

Once I had my tea, Newt headed for the door. At first, I thought he was leaving, but instead he just hung his high-vis jacket on the coat rack.

"You don't have to stick around," I said when I realized he had no intention of leaving any time soon. "I'll be fine."

Newt sat beside me again, looking at something on his phone. "I'm not going anywhere. You can barely walk right now. There's nothing wrong with needing help when you're injured. I don't mind... oh."

I set aside my empty mug, placing it on the floor since there was no table in the small space. "Oh?"

In an odd show of annoyance, Newt glared at the mug as if it had insulted his family lineage. "Oolong has caffeine."

"All right. And..."

"Caffeine hinders bone growth. You shouldn't have that."

"I'm sure one time won't hurt." I ran my hand through my hair and scowled at the oily texture. "Besides, I'm going to need the energy to take a shower.”

Newt jumped up so quickly, one would think the couch had burned him. “No, you can’t do that. You can’t get your cast wet.”

“Well, I’m not staying like this.” I gestured at my disheveled state. “I feel gross.”

For a moment, Newt looked like he was going to argue but then a thoughtful look came over his face.

“Let me take a look at your bathroom.”

He disappeared, and I could hear him moving around in the other room muttering to himself. Then, a few moments later, he returned with a grin and a trash bag.

“All right. Here’s what we’ll do. Luckily, you have a bathtub. You can take a bath, so long as we prop your leg up out of the water and wrap the cast in this bag.”

It wasn’t ideal, but I would take what I could get so long as I was clean by the end of it.

Moving me from the couch to the bathroom turned out to be a trial worthy of Hercules. When I furnished the apartment, I’d been more concerned with getting everything I needed in one apartment, and less concerned with walking space. Mobility had never been an issue.

By the time I was sitting on the closed toilet lid next to the tub, I was already out of breath.

Newt made sure to lean my crutches against the wall within grabbing distance. "I'll get the water ready. You get undressed."

My breath immediately returned when Newt bent over the tub to inspect the faucet handles, and I was treated to a great view of his ass. I lingered for a moment, enjoying the sight, but turned my attention to the task of undressing before I could get too excited.

I was really liking this bossy side of him.

Removing my shirt and shoes was no problem, but my pants proved a bit more difficult. I needed to stand to get them off, but in order to stand, I needed to hold onto my crutch. The only option would be to balance solely on my good leg without the crutch so my hands would be free, but that seemed like a recipe for disaster.

When Newt glanced back over and saw me sitting there still half-clothed, he immediately guessed the problem.

"Stand up. I'll do it."

Taking hold of my crutch, I hoisted myself back onto my feet. "I get it. This whole thing is just a ploy to see me naked." I flashed him a grin.

With surprisingly deft fingers, Newt undid my pants. They fell to the floor along with my boxers, leaving my body on full display. I wasn't normally self-conscious. I worked out a lot and it showed. However, no amount of muscle could compensate for the battered state the car crash had left me in. Large dark bruises marred my skin, and angry wounds were stitched together with black thread.

I expected Newt to pull back. Surely, even a nurse would find such a sight ugly. Yet surprisingly, his blue eyes sparkled with heat when he looked up at me through long lashes.

"It's been a hard week. I deserve to get something fun out of all this."

Yes, I was definitely liking this bossy side of Newt, and despite my injuries, my cock twitched with interest.

However, Newt seemed to have reached the end of his confidence. He looked away, blushing deeply, as if even he couldn't believe what he'd just said.

"Let's, um... let's get you in the tub."

I gripped the edge of the tub, preparing for the struggle of climbing in, when an idea occurred to me. Smirking, I looked over my shoulder at Newt.

"You know, trying to take a bath with my leg propped up on the edge is going to be difficult. It would be easier if you joined me."

Just in case my intention wasn't clear, I let my gaze drag up and down Newt's body. The other man wasn't the only one who deserved a reward after such a disastrous week.

Newt's hands clutched the front of his shirt and his blush burned so brightly I feared his face would catch fire.

"You mean, get in the bath with you?"

Rather than reply with words, I merely raised an eyebrow and nodded at the tub.

Steam gathered in the bathroom as Newt considered what to do, biting his lip as if chewing his thoughts. Then, nodding to himself, he quickly pulled off his shirt and let it fall to the floor.

Just as I'd imagined, his blush did travel over his chest. It turned his pale skin a rosy pink all the way from his collarbone to his nipples. To my even greater delight, more freckles decorated his shoulders just like they did his cheeks. I wanted to count them with my lips, kissing each one until I'd cataloged every spot.

Newt stood in the middle of the bathroom with his arms wrapped around his stomach. He was obviously self-conscious, and that couldn't be allowed to continue.

I pulled him into my arms, keeping one hand braced against the wall to avoid leaning all my weight on him, and buried my face in his hair.

"Almost makes crashing off a bridge worth it if this is my reward."

One of Newt's hands slapped against my chest, barely making contact, before he wrapped both arms around my waist. "Don't joke about that."

I slid my hand down his back, inching it toward the waistband of his pants.

"Fine. No jokes. We can just focus on this instead."

At the word "this" I slipped my hand inside his pants and squeezed his ass.

Newt squealed and jumped, nearly

knocking us both over.

I grabbed onto the sink for balance and luckily, managed to stay upright.

"Are you trying to give me a heart attack," he yelled, slapping me again. This time he almost hit me for real.

Unconcerned, I tugged at the front of his pants. "No, I'm trying to get you naked. You got to see all of me. It's only polite to return the favor."

His arms crossed over his chest, hiding his cute pink nipples from my sight. "You're ridiculous."

I tugged at his pants again. "I'm also insistent. Come on."

With a sigh and a roll of his eyes, Newt gave in and removed his pants. We finally stood together in the bathroom's limited space, bare of all obstacles between us.

This time Newt's blush traveled even farther than his chest, reaching all the way down to his stomach. The muscles just above his navel quivered.

I wanted to bite them.

I sighed. Another time.

Right now, I wouldn't be able to bend down that far.

Instead, I took his face in my hands and looked directly into those beautiful blue eyes. "Perfect."

Then I pressed my lips to his, and Newt responded with equal fervor. He opened his lips, so our mouths slotted together as close as possible and his tongue pushed against mine, inviting me to come play.

Unfortunately, my one-legged balance didn't allow us to stay this way for long. After only a minute, I was ready to fall over, so we had to part.

With Newt's help, I wrapped my cast in a trash bag and lowered myself into the tub. Once I was settled, Newt joined me. He sat behind me, supporting my body so that I could lie back without letting my leg slip into the water. Our size difference made for a comical sight. He could barely see over my shoulder, but we managed to get comfortable.

Closing my eyes, I listened to Newt humming under his breath as he ran a washcloth over my skin and rubbed shampoo into my hair. I couldn't decide what felt better, the other man's hands on my skin, or the relief of finally getting clean.

The pleasant sensation came to an abrupt halt as Newt's hands suddenly froze on my belly. He'd been steadily making his way down my body but seemed to realize he was about to cross a line.

"Do you want to do the rest yourself?"

His hand stayed in place, lingering just above my navel as he waited for my answer.

Finding the right words was never my strongest talent, especially in unusual situations. I had plenty of experience with sex, but intimacy not so much.

Rather than risk saying the wrong thing and disrupting the atmosphere we'd created, I responded by grabbing his hand and sliding it farther down.

This was apparently exactly the green light he was looking for because he didn't hesitate again. His hand dipped between my legs, teasing the flesh there before finally grasping my half-hard arousal.

I gasped and writhed, letting out a soft moan as he started to stroke me, but his other hand pressed against my chest to keep me leaning back against him.

"Relax," he whispered in my ear. "I've got you."

It was the sweetest, most tender hand-job I'd ever received. The hot water of the bath kept my muscles loose as Newt slowly guided me toward a much-anticipated orgasm. Little by little, with each movement of his hand, pleasure twisted in my stomach. Yet, the sensation never turned sharp or explosive as it usually did for me. Instead, when I tipped over the edge of my climax, it felt more like the relief of a knotted muscle finally releasing.

Even after it ended, I continued to float in the water as Newt finished cleaning me up. My bones, both the healthy ones and the broken ones, felt like they had been replaced with Jello. The good news was that nothing hurt anymore. The bad news was that I wouldn't be able to move any time soon.

"Just leave me here," I said when Newt stood up and tried to coax me out of the tub. "I can sleep here until everything is healed."

Hooking his hands under my arms, Newt forced me to stand up. "Come on. You'll be much more comfortable in a proper bed."

He was surprisingly strong for his size, and supported the majority of my weight as I climbed out of the tub and wrapped myself in a bathrobe. It was probably a result of his jobs since both nurses and paramedics needed to physically assist patients.

Lucky for me, because even with the aid of a crutch, I could barely walk straight as I made my way to my bedroom.

It wasn't much. There was just enough space for a bed, table, and a television, but it served my needs just fine. I was even glad for the small space when Newt was forced to sit on the bed beside me. He'd stolen one of my T-shirts since his own clothes had ended up wet on the bathroom floor. The shirt was large enough to fall to mid-thigh on him, but rode up when he leaned against me, showing off most of his legs.

"Feeling better?"

Before I could speak, my stomach answered for me and let out a loud grumble. The hospital food wasn't particularly appetizing, so I hadn't eaten much over the last few days.

Embarrassment made my ears feel hot, but Newt just laughed and patted my arm.

"I'll make you some food. It's time for

you to take your pain meds anyway."

Before heading to the kitchen, he first made sure my leg was supported on all sides by pillows and that I was sitting comfortably with my back against the headboard.

I couldn't remember the last time I'd been pampered in such a way. When I was a kid, my parents had taken care of me whenever I was sick or injured, but it had been so long since they died that remembering them now felt like watching someone else's life.

Since their death, Damien and I had done our best to take care of each other, but for so many years our goal was to simply stay alive. Comfort hadn't been a priority.

While Newt was in the kitchen, I dozed off, drifting through a mix of scrambled memories. I awoke to the feeling of a hand on my shoulder, with the sound of a gunshot echoing in my ears and the scent of blood in my nose.

"Woah," Newt gasped when I instinctively knocked his hand away. "Sorry. Didn't mean to startle you. Here. You need to eat something."

I stared blankly at the bowl of soup he

handed me. Old memories faded behind my eyes, and I focused on the present.

There was no blood. No mafia goons with guns. Everyone was safe.

I sucked in a deep breath and took the bowl of soup, thanking Newt for his effort, but I regretted it the moment I took the first sip and nearly choked.

"Ugh. What is this? It's worse than hospital food."

Newt sat back down at my side and absently adjusted a few of the pillows. "Sorry. It was the only thing I could find in your kitchen without sodium. Too much salt isn't good for you when you're healing. I'll stop at the store tomorrow and get you some better options."

"Don't worry about it. Just give Damien a list and he'll go get it." I stared down at the unappealing liquid filling my bowl. "So, is this what the next few weeks of my life are going to be like? Nothing but health food?"

When I continued to hold a staring contest with my meal rather than eating it, Newt nudged the bowl closer. "Until you're better, yes. Now, eat up. You need to take your pills."

Forgoing the spoon altogether, I

brought the bowl to my lips and chugged the soup all at once. Luckily, it was a very thin broth so I didn't choke. After it was gone, I immediately downed a glass of water along with my prescribed meds, but the aftertaste lingered on my tongue.

"Come here." I tugged Newt closer. "I need something to wash the taste out."

"I can get you more water."

"No. I have a better idea."

Before he could protest, I yanked my shirt off of him, then slid down the bed until I was lying flat on my back.

Newt wrapped his arms around his legs, hiding his suddenly naked body as he looked at me in confusion. "What are you doing?"

"Getting comfortable. Now come here. You've been doing so much to take care of me, I should reward you."

He still seemed confused, but followed my directions as I guided him to kneel over my head.

"Are you sure about this?" His fingers gripped tightly to the headboard, and he looked down at me with wide eyes.

I grinned. "Absolutely."

Taking hold of his hips, I positioned him so I could easily take his cock into my mouth without having to strain my neck.

The headboard rattled above me as Newt gripped it tighter. "Oh, you're... Okay, we're doing this." He sucked in a deep breath and let out a hiss as I enveloped the head of his dick in my mouth, groaning as the taste of him graced my tongue and exploded in my mouth from the pearl of pre-cum on his slit

Laughing to myself, I hummed my appreciation around the flesh in my mouth before swallowing his shaft deeper. Newt whined and tried to buck his hips, but I held on tight. This time, we were going at my pace.

I kept it slow, teasing him with my lips and tongue as I drew him in and out of my mouth. Although I couldn't see Newt's expression, I could tell he was losing his mind from the way he kept babbling.

"Oh, please. More. No... I don't. Yes. Like that."

He never cursed like many people did during sex. Not even when his legs began to shake, and I could tell he was hanging on by a thread. He begged and pleaded with broken sentences, but not a single swear word slipped from his lips.

I kept it up as long as I could, bringing him right to the brink of orgasm before backing off, until his begging changed into kitten-like mewls. His thighs shook on either side of my head, and his hips twitched in sporadic little thrusts that didn't go anywhere.

To put it simply, he was desperate.

It was just what I wanted.

Taking a deep breath, I swallowed him all the way to the root. He was just large enough to strain the muscles of my throat without choking me, and I let my tongue run over the sensitive underside of his cock.

He moaned long and low when he erupted down my throat, practically collapsing against the headboard. I swallowed everything he had to give me, and even lapped up any drops that escaped me initially.

It was certainly a better meal than the soup had been.

As soon as he could move, Newt crawled off me and flopped over in a pile of tangled limbs.

"That was..." He trailed off, too busy panting to bother with words. His face was flushed an even brighter red than his hair and sweat beaded along his forehead.

It was too bad I didn't have a camera. I would have loved to take a picture of Newt's satisfied expression at that moment.

I pulled the younger man closer, dragging him across the mattress when he couldn't coordinate enough to move on his own, and tucked him against my side. Throwing a blanket over both of us, I decided a nap was in order. It had been a long week, and we were both physically and emotionally exhausted.

There were plenty of things we needed to worry about, but they could wait. As I drifted off to sleep, the only thought in my mind was the idea of watching a movie with Newt later. Unlike when I watched anything with Damien, neither of us would have to give in to the other's demands, because we both had the same preferences in entertainment.

So long as Newt didn't want to watch The Little Mermaid, then we'd be fine.

CHAPTER ELEVEN

Newt

"I DON'T WANT to do this," I whined into my phone.

"I know." Frankie's voice consoled me from the other end of the line. "But you promised to meet your sister for lunch a month ago, and you know how she gets when you cancel plans with her at the last minute. Just go, smile and nod for an hour or two, then you can get back to your injured boyfriend."

It was an average Saturday afternoon in Baton Rouge, which meant the sidewalks weren't too crowded even on a day with perfect weather. I walked along the road, paying more attention to my phone than my feet.

"He's not my boyfriend. We haven't had that conversation yet."

Frankie scoffed so audibly I could hear it over the line. "Please. For weeks now, you've spent every moment you aren't working at his apartment playing nursemaid. You're definitely boyfriends at this point."

I couldn't even argue. Everything he said was true. For the last three weeks, I'd practically lived with Sebastian. The cast on his leg made mobility difficult, and his brother was busy trying to find whoever ran him off the road. He needed someone around, and I was happy to fill that role.

Whether or not that made us an official couple, however, was still up for debate, but I didn't feel like tackling that argument.

"Actually, Frankie, I could use some advice. What are some safe exercises Bastian could do to stay active? I can tell he's getting stir crazy, and there's only so much I can do to keep him occupied."

"What? The sex getting boring already?"

Blood rushed to my face as I

remembered everything Sebastian and I had gotten up to over the last few weeks. We'd explored every kind of position that kept Sebastian's leg supported, but there was one thing we hadn't done yet.

"Shut up. Don't remind me. We haven't even gone all the way yet. I've had more sex in the last few weeks than in my entire life, but I'm still so horny."

I shouted a little too loud and several people on the sidewalk looked at me with judging eyes. Keeping my gaze on my feet, I walked faster.

Frankie's laughter trickled out of the phone directly into my ear. "Really. After all this time, he still hasn't fucked you yet?"

"With his injuries, we can't do anything too stressful. I'm just glad he likes giving blowjobs as much as receiving them, so I don't have to do all the work."

The restaurant where I agreed to have lunch with my sister loomed up ahead, but I hung back and pretended to look at a window display. There were still ten minutes before I needed to meet her and I refused to be early.

On the other side of the phone, I heard the ding of our microwave as Frankie made himself lunch.

"A generous lover. I'm jealous. The last guy I slept with expected me to just let him stick it in without any foreplay. He was hot too. I've never been so disappointed."

I rolled my eyes, having heard this story a dozen times before. "And that's why we both agreed not to sleep with someone on the first date anymore. It never works out well."

"You can't talk. You and Bastian have only had one official date, and that one barely counts, yet you're already acting like you're on your honeymoon."

Although he couldn't see me, I stuck my tongue out at him. Unfortunately, I forgot I was standing in front of a window display, so it looked like I'd made the rude face at a woman inside the shop.

Our gazes locked through the glass, and she scowled. I tried to mouth an apology to her, but it must not have translated because she got even more visibly upset. Giving up, I scurried away from the shop before the woman decided to confront me.

"Anyway, I didn't call just to gossip about my sex life. I really need some suggestions for Bastian. I caught him trying to work out the other day. He nearly dropped a dumbbell on his foot."

Not to mention the multiple times he'd tried returning to work. I'd already had to stop him from leaving the apartment when he decided to try continuing the search for Clay Dahler. Sure, a missing person case may be safer than hunting down a pedophile ring. However, until we knew for sure who tried to kill him—running him off the road had not just been a warning, it was an attempt on his life—he needed to stay inside where people couldn't get to him.

I sighed, remembering the argument the brothers had gotten into when Sebastian was caught trying to break into Damien's computer. It had been an ugly sight. The pair didn't argue often, but when they did, they held nothing back.

"Bastian really shouldn't be getting worked up right now. I need to give him something safe to do, but I don't know what would be best. I treat injuries. I don't usually handle the recovery process. That's your area of expertise."

Frankie hummed as he thought for a moment, and I could hear him munching on whatever he'd chosen for lunch.

"It's hard to say without seeing him myself. Would it be possible for me to come over and evaluate him? I could give you some better suggestions then."

I'd reached the restaurant and it was almost time to meet my sister. There were no more excuses I could use to delay the inevitable.

"I'll ask, but I don't see why you couldn't come over. I've got to go now, but I'll give you a call later."

"Sure. Have fun and try not to give your sister anything to complain about. You'll only make it worse for yourself."

I hung up and stored my phone in my pocket. Then, with a deep breath, I opened the door to the restaurant.

Holy Trinity Bistro claimed to be an authentic Creole restaurant. It certainly had the vibe down, presenting a mix of homey yet elegant. The name was a reference to the three staple ingredients in Creole cooking, onion, celery, and green bell pepper. I was convinced that the name had been chosen to hide the fact that the chefs didn't actually know what they were doing. Half of the items on the menu weren't even Creole recipes, and the items that were authentic were comically stereotypical. It was like someone had looked up a list of recipes off the Internet and decided to just give it a try.

However, it was one of my sister's favorite restaurants, so that's where we ended up going whenever we got lunch together.

I wouldn't mind our occasional lunches if it wasn't for what came with them.

"Hey, midget. How you doing?"

A man waved at me from where he had an arm slung over my sister's shoulder.

Dean Barrett was my sister's fiancé. They'd been dating for nearly ten years, so I'd known him for a significant amount of my life. Yet, even after all that time, I still didn't really like him.

"Hey, Dean," I said, giving him the simplest greeting I could get away with.

He reached out for me, and I braced myself as he ruffled my hair hard enough to rock my head back and forth.

"Man, this is getting long. You need to get a haircut soon or people are going to start mistaking you for a girl."

I ran a hand over my hair, trying to smooth it back into place. "Uh, I'll keep that in mind."

A more blatant lie had never left my lips. I absolutely would not even think about cutting my hair. After finding out how much Sebastian liked its length, especially during sex since it gave him something to hold onto, I was never cutting my hair again.

Well, maybe if it got too long. An image of myself as Rapunzel popped into my mind. If my hair ever got that long, then I would cut it, but it would never be short enough for Dean's preference.

I eyed his neatly trimmed crew cut.

No, never that short.

My attention was diverted when my sister pulled me into a hug. "Newton. I'm glad you came."

After so many years, I'd given up trying to get her to stop using my full name. Instead, I kept the complaint to myself and hugged her back. "Hi, Rosalind. Of course I came. I promised, after all."

Rosalind was taller than me by several inches, so when she pulled back, she had to look down to meet my eyes.

"It's been too long since we last spoke. Tell me what's been going on with you?" Dean tapped her on the shoulder, and they held a silent conversation with their eyes before she seemed to remember something. "Oh, right. Newton, there's someone I want you to meet. This is Steven, Dean's cousin. He'll be joining us today."

They directed my attention to a younger man standing just behind them that I hadn't even noticed at first. He had a slightly mousy look, with a mop of brown hair that fell over his forehead, and thick glasses perched on his nose.

"Hi," he said, looking somewhere just over my shoulder rather than meeting my eye.

"Um, hi." I reached out to shake his hand, but he didn't take it, so I was left standing awkwardly with my hand in the air.

"Steven just moved to Baton Rouge," Rosalind said when it became clear that Steven and I needed someone to rescue the conversation. "Since he's new here, he doesn't know many people in the city, so I thought it would be a good idea to invite him along."

"All right," I said, not knowing how else to respond. It was unusual. They didn't usually invite other people on these little lunch dates, but if Steven was Dean's cousin that technically made him family.

A waiter showed us to our table, where Rosalind and Dean ended up sitting on one side while Steven and I sat on the other. At least this time we'd managed to get a table by the window, so I had something to look at. The restaurant had a great view of a nearby river. Sunlight glinted off the water as people sailed by in small boats just below us.

After the waiter took our drink orders, Rosalind turned her full attention on me. "So, Newton, what have you been up to?"

There were plenty of things I could tell her about. The burned John Doe that we still hadn't identified, everything with Sebastian, or even just an interesting call I'd gone out on the other day with Firehouse Twenty-One where I helped rescue a kid from a tree that was simultaneously on fire. We still hadn't figured out how the tree ended up on fire at the same time the kid was stuck in it, though we suspected fireworks had been involved.

However, I'd attended enough of these lunches with my sister to know the script.

"Oh, nothing much. Work keeps me

pretty busy."

"I know exactly what you mean," Rosalind agreed. "Between wedding planning and this new case my firm has taken on, I feel run ragged most days."

As usual, most of the conversation became a rant about my sister's work, punctuated by bits of info about the upcoming wedding. Rosalind was a lawyer at a fairly successful firm, and she never missed an opportunity to bring it up. I couldn't be too mad. She'd worked hard for her career and should be proud. However, I did get tired of listening to the same topics over and over again.

Not to mention the little passive aggressive comments that inevitably slipped into the conversation.

"All those years of law school were hard, but I'm so glad I stuck with it. Have you considered going back to school, Newton? You really would make a great doctor."

"We're looking into buying a house, so we'll be ready to start a family once we're married. Are you still sharing an apartment with that roommate of yours? What's his name? Frank?"

"It's so strange. Wedding planning has

been a nightmare, but also rewarding at the same time. I suppose that doesn't make sense to you now, but you'll understand when you're planning your own wedding."

Each little comment, said in a way that made it hard to argue, felt like a needle wedging under my ribs. My life didn't align with what my sister envisioned for me. She meant well, but she had a very narrow view of what was "best". To her, anything less than a high paying job, white picket fence, kids, and an arm-candy husband was a wasted life.

Well, that was an unfair description of Dean. I may not like the guy, but he was at least successful in his own way. He was an aspiring actor and had landed a few parts in several successful films. They were generic action movies, most of which I had never seen, but they did pay well. He'd have no problem keeping up with my sister's financial goals for their future.

My sister had been talking for several minutes, and the waiter had already come by to take our orders, when Steven suddenly turned to me.

"So, Newton. You work at a hospital, right?"

SEBASTIAN

He'd been so quiet up until now, I'd almost forgotten about him and wasn't ready for the unexpected question. It was a generic conversation topic, but at least it was better than listening to my sister's passive aggressive judgment of my life.

"Yeah, I'm a nurse, and I'm also a paramedic." I flashed him a fake half-smile, trying to appear like I was interested in a conversation with him.

His hand shook slightly as he pushed his glasses back into place on his nose. "Oh, wow. Two jobs. That must be tough."

I thought over everything my jobs had brought me recently, both the good and the bad. "Yeah, but it's worth it. What about you?"

He opened his mouth as if about to speak, but immediately closed it again. After several moments, he mumbled something so quietly I had no idea what he said.

Rosalind interjected herself into the conversation and answered for him. "Steven just got a job at that cafe you like, Newton. You know, the one with all the weird decorations."

She could only be talking about one place. Despite her unflattering description, a smile lit my face. "Oh, you work at Cool Beans. I love it there."

The cafe held a special spot in my heart, especially since it had hosted my first and only date with Sebastian.

How could I not smile when thinking about it?

Steven's fingers nervously twisted the straw of his drink into knots, but he managed a small smile of his own. "Do you go there a lot?"

"Yeah. It's right down the street from the hospital, so I go there all the time. It's great."

"I like it too. The owner lets me read the comic books on my breaks. He even showed me some golden age Justice League comics."

With that, we'd finally managed to find a topic of conversation we could both enjoy. Steven was a diehard DC fan, while I'd always enjoyed both DC and Marvel equally. It wasn't like the two were exclusive, and I saw no reason to limit my choices. However, it was fun to take the stance of arguing for Marvel over DC just for the sake of debate. Especially, since Steven didn't get mad whenever I disagreed with him, like some fans would.

Rosalind and Dean seemed happy to let us talk and occupied themselves with their own wedding discussions. The debate of Marvel versus DC led into a conversation about which comic book movies we thought were the most successful in adapting their source material. We could easily agree on which ones had failed, but differed when it came to our opinions on success. He argued that it was only a success if the movie stuck to the original storyline, whereas I was less concerned with plot so long as the movie captured the heart of the characters.

This conversation lasted us most of the way through lunch. I was glad to see that Steven wasn't as standoffish as he first seemed. Once he got over his initial shyness, he was actually pleasant company.

I had just finished the last bite of my crab cakes when Steven's tone suddenly changed.

"Hey, Newton. I wanted to apologize if I was awkward earlier. I'm not very good at this, so thanks for understanding."

My mouth was still full, making me resemble my chipmunk nickname more than usual. I used the excuse of swallowing and taking a sip of water to buy myself time. Something about his choice of words struck me as odd.

"Not good at what? Lunch?" I laughed, hoping to play it off as a joke.

Yet, Steven's serious tone remained.

"No, I'm not good at dating. I always get so nervous on first dates that I end up making a fool of myself, or just not saying anything at all. But this one has gone much better than usual."

My brain stalled, and for a moment I heard nothing but the sound of an old dialup Internet connection.

"I'm sorry. What did you say? Date?"

I didn't give him time to answer, instead directing my demands at my sister. "Rosalind. Is this a setup for a date?"

My blood boiled, and my pleasant meal sat like ash in my stomach.

Yet, Rosalind just waved her hand like my anger could be simply brushed aside. "Oh, come on, Newton. You need to get out there and start dating. You'll be much happier with a partner in your life. I'm just helping you out."

My teeth grated against each other,

and I gripped my fork hard enough to leave an impression of the handle against my palm. "You should have asked me first. I'm already seeing someone. If my boyfriend finds out I went on a date with someone else, who knows what he'll think."

Earlier, I'd questioned if Sebastian and I even counted as boyfriends, but now the word slipped easily from my mouth.

I couldn't even look at Steven. There was probably a lot of hurt and confusion on his face that I couldn't bear to see. He was a decent man who didn't deserve the situation my sister had put him in.

Rosalind, on the other hand, didn't even look ashamed. In fact, she only got more excited.

"Oh, Newton. You're seeing someone? Why didn't you tell me?"

If this were a cartoon, steam would have been spewing out of my ears like a pair of tea kettles. "Because you aren't entitled to front row tickets to my private life. And after this little stunt, I don't think I'm going to tell you anything ever again."

"Hold on," Dean interrupted my tirade. "Are you really dating someone? You've never managed to get past a first date for as long as I've known you, and now suddenly, you have a boyfriend? Who is this person?"

I didn't usually curse, but this situation called for it. There was no choice. I had to either tell them about Sebastian or look like a liar.

Still glaring at my sister and Dean, I pulled out my phone. I'd taken several pictures of Sebastian over the last few weeks, but most of them were from after he'd been injured. He would never want those images to be someone's first impression of him. There was only one picture on my phone from before the car crash, which I had taken during our date at the coffee shop.

This was the picture I handed over to them. "His name is Bastian. I met him at the hospital when he came to check in on a patient."

My sister's eyes grew large when she looked at my screen, and Dean even let out a little "Woah."

At first I thought they were impressed with the sight of Sebastian. It was an understandable reaction. He was an impressive man.

However, I turned out to be wrong when Dean started laughing.

"Seriously? You're trying to claim that you're dating this guy? Newton, man, if you're going to lie at least make it believable."

My sister didn't laugh. Instead, she shook her head in disappointment. "Newton, you shouldn't take pictures of people without their consent. You need to get rid of this."

Her finger swiped across the screen, opening the tab to delete the photo.

I grabbed the phone from her before she could hit the "yes" option.

"I'm not lying, and don't mess with my phone."

The pitiful looks they gave me made my skin crawl, and I already knew there was no point arguing with them. Nothing I said would convince them that I was telling the truth.

Part of the problem was the picture itself. I'd snapped it covertly while we were at the coffee shop so that I could have an image to remember him by just in case the date didn't go well. That meant I wasn't in the photo with him, and he wasn't even looking at the screen. It really did look like I'd just taken a picture of some random stranger.

It was no wonder they didn't believe I was dating Sebastian. Sometimes, I couldn't even believe it myself.

"Whatever," I said as I shoved my phone back in my pocket. "I don't owe you an explanation. Believe what you want. I'm done." I was about to storm out when I noticed the crushed look on Steven's face. "Hey, um, I'm sorry about this. You're a great guy, and you didn't deserve this. I hope your next date goes better."

I tried to leave with my dignity intact, but my sister ran after me.

"Newton. Wait."

I kept walking, all the way out the door and onto the sidewalk. Her footsteps echoed behind me, so I headed for the crosswalk to try and put distance between us.

Two steps off the curb, she caught my arm. "Newton. Wait. Talk to me."

I slapped her hand away, hard enough for the sound of skin striking skin to echo off the cars waiting at the light.

"What's there to talk about? How you manipulated me? How you lied to me? God, I have never been so mortified in my life as I am right now."

She reached out like she would grab me again but changed her mind. "You're right. I should have asked you first, but every time I've suggested people for you to date in the past you've always turned me down. You and Steven have a lot in common, and I think you'd do well together."

"Except for the fact that I'm already seeing someone. That would probably throw a monkey wrench in the relationship."

The pity was back in her eyes. She still thought I was lying.

"Newton—"

I cut her off.

"No. Don't even start. You've got all these plans for what you think my life should be, but how can you know what's best for me when you can't even get my name right. It's Newt. Not Newton. I hate my full name. You know that, yet you insist on using it anyway."

Now she looked angry. In that moment, I knew how the opposing lawyers must feel when they had to face her across a courtroom.

"Newt is a child's name. You're an

adult. You need to act like it. Now stop this tantrum and come back inside the restaurant so we discuss this like adults."

I turned and kept walking toward the other side of the street. "I'm not discussing anything with people who think I'm a liar."

"Newton." Her voice was more distressed than before.

"Leave me alone," I shouted over my shoulder.

"Newt."

The sound of my preferred name made me pause.

If I'd kept walking, I would have died right there on that street.

Rosalind grabbed me by the shirt and yanked me backward. We both went tumbling over the pavement, right before a car barreled past. Its front fender missed me by inches. It didn't even try to stop or slow down. At the next intersection, it swerved around the corner so quickly that its wheels let out a painful squeal. Then it completed the turn and disappeared from sight.

I stared down the road in shock, even after the car was long gone.

Rosalind's hands ran over me,

searching for injuries. "Oh my god. Newton. Are you okay? That guy must have been drunk or something. He just ran right through the red light."

The more frantic she became, the more my thoughts calmed.

A picture started to form in my mind.

"Hey, Rosalind? What color was that car?"

"Why does that matter?" She pulled me to my feet. "Come on. Let's get out of the road."

I let her lead me but persisted with my question. "Just answer. What color was it?"

"Um, black." She checked me over again. "Are you sure you're okay?"

"I'm fine. Did you see who was driving?"

She grabbed my face and stared directly into my eyes. "You're acting weird. Did you hit your head? Maybe we should call someone."

My calm facade cracked, and I snapped at her. "Just answer the question."

Something in my expression must have startled her because she actually listened to me.

"No, I didn't see the driver. The windows were blacked out. If I had seen them, I'd be reporting them right now."

Right after Sebastian was attacked, Damien had managed to get a hold of the video from his dashcam. It didn't show much, since the camera pointed forward, and the cars that drove him off the road stayed mostly to the sides and behind. However, it had gotten one clear picture of the attackers' cars driving away right before Sebastian went over the edge of the bridge.

I'd been there when Sebastian and Damien reviewed the footage, and clearly remembered the long scrape on the side of one of the cars. When it slammed into Sebastian's car, black paint had been scraped away revealing the metal underneath. The twisted silver streak stretched all the way from the passenger door to the rear taillight and stood out starkly on the black backdrop.

The car that almost hit me a moment ago had the exact same scrape down its side.

"I need to go."

Rosalind called my name, but I ignored her as I started running down the road in the direction of Sebastian's apartment.

Maybe I was being paranoid, but it seemed like one of the cars that ran Sebastian off the road had just tried to kill me as well.

CHAPTER TWELVE

Sebastian

"SEBASTIAN, WHAT ARE you doing?"

I looked up from my precarious position to see Damien standing in the doorway with a disappointed scowl on his face.

The whole world was upside down from my view on the floor. I'd decided to try working out. My leg and my ribs were still injured, but my arms were fine. Surely a few bench presses wouldn't hurt. Lying on the bench had proven difficult when I couldn't bend my leg to touch the ground, so I'd constructed a makeshift hammock out of a towel and several ropes to support my cast.

It had worked better than I hoped, but I unfortunately forgot about the hammock when I stood up. The resulting disaster left me splayed over the floor with ropes tangled around my leg.

This was, of course, the exact moment Damien walked in the door.

Sighing deeply, he helped me disentangle myself and sat me down on the couch.

"Sebastian, you can't be doing these things. Especially not when you're alone. Where's Newt?"

I leaned back and draped one arm over my eyes to hide my embarrassment.

"He's having lunch with his sister. Just because I'm on house arrest doesn't mean he should be."

Damien sighed again, and I listened to his footsteps on the floorboards as he moved closer.

"This isn't a punishment, Bas." The cushions dipped as he sat next to me and pressed my crutch into my hand. "You're healing. Severe injuries like yours take time and you need to..." He trailed off, and the atmosphere around us grew tense.

SEBASTIAN

Too late, I remembered the laptop I'd left open on the arm of the couch. Lunging across Damien, I tried to grab the device, but he held it out of my reach.

"Sebastian, what is this?"

"It's nothing." I tried to grab it again, but he held me back with a single hand on my chest. Normally, I could have put up more of a fight, the two of us were equal in strength, but my ribs still ached, and my muscles felt weak after three weeks of sitting around.

He barely had to glance at the info on my laptop to know exactly what I'd been up to.

"You're still searching for Clay Dahler?"

I gave up fighting and sat up straight. My crutch slid from its position leaning against the couch seat and banged against my good leg. Glaring at it, I balanced the metal stick against the arm of the couch instead.

"Yeah. Figured I could make myself useful somehow. But it's useless. I've exhausted every lead I can think of and found nothing. The man may as well not exist."

"He's been missing for almost ten

years. We both knew finding him after so much time would be a long shot."

The crutch fell again, this time nearly knocking into my injured leg. I caught it just in time, but the feel of the cool metal under my hand enraged me. This thing was supposed to help me.

Couldn't it do at least one thing right, like staying where I put it?

Shouting in frustration, I threw the crutch away. It hit the floor and skidded a few feet before bouncing off the wall where it left a dent in the plaster.

"I just... fuck. I should at least be able to do this much. Even if I can't get out there and look for myself, finding some information for you to follow shouldn't be so hard."

Damien said nothing about my outburst as he set my laptop aside. "So, when your investigation turned up empty, you decided to try exercising?"

I nodded and hunched forward so my face landed in my hands.

Damien inhaled deeply through his nose, then held his breath for a moment. When he finally exhaled, the air came out in one decisive snort, like a bull getting ready to charge.

"All right. I wasn't going to get you involved, but at this point if I leave you alone, you're just going to hurt yourself even more. I'm meeting some members of the FPA in our office soon. If you'd like, you can join me."

I immediately rose from my slump. My ribs protested the quick movement, but I didn't care. "Mason wouldn't be meeting with you unless it was important. What happened?"

"While looking into the child disappearances, I've been focusing on the adoption agencies the women claimed to have given their children to."

"Yeah, I looked at those as well." In fact, I'd spent so long looking into the adoption agencies that the information was practically branded on my eyeballs. "They all seem to be legit organizations."

Damien nodded. "They are. A false adoption agency would eventually draw attention, so I figured whoever is taking these children must be using real adoption agencies as a cover. So, I looked at the employee records, and I found one man who volunteers at two of the agencies where children went missing."

"What? No. I've combed through those

records so carefully. I wouldn't have missed something so obvious." I shook my head, my shoulders drooping. I couldn't believe I hadn't found that. Normally, I'd never miss something so potentially important.

What was wrong with me?

Ugh. Fuck.

"The man's name is Smith Harper. I almost missed the connection as well, because of the way the two organizations file their employee info. One lists the names with first name followed by surname, while the other agency lists the names with the surname first. Different formatting like this usually isn't a problem, but with Smith Harper, where both names could be either first name or surname, it's easy to overlook."

It couldn't be that simple.

I'd been spinning my wheels on this case for months, all because of paperwork formatting?

Goddamn it!

I wanted to shout and cry at the same time, maybe punch a wall for good measure, but there was nothing left to throw, and I couldn't afford any more injuries. In the end, all I could do was clench my fists until my nails bit crescents into my palms.

"So, we've got a name. Great. What do we know about this Smith Harper, other than the fact that the name is probably an alias?"

"I don't know. Once I found a connection between two of the adoption agencies, I turned the information over to the FPA."

I started to argue, but Damien was already raising his hand to silence me.

"Don't even start. I know you want to handle this case, but the FPA has a lot more resources than us. They can get answers faster, and in the end that's all that matters. Right? The point is to protect the children, not stroke our own egos, and the best way to protect the children is to stop the bad guys as soon as possible."

I still wanted to argue but could think of nothing else to say. All I could do was wave an accusatory finger in his face. "I hate when you use logic against me. It's not fair."

Finally, for the first time since Damien stepped into the room, he smiled. "No, it's entirely fair. That's why you're so mad.

Now, come on. We're meeting with Mason's guys soon, and it's going to take us all day just to get you down the stairs." He fetched my crutches from the other side of the room.

My hand wrapped around the familiar handle, and I hoisted myself onto my feet. I already dreaded the short but difficult journey ahead of me.

When Damien said he had a meeting with members of the FPA "soon", it apparently meant "right now".

We made our way down to our office on the lower floor, taking several minutes to navigate my crutches on the stairs, only to find a pair of agents already waiting for us.

One of them I recognized.

Gabe Long.

The man was a FBI agent on loan to the FPA but he still worked out of his old FBI office on cases too. I still didn't truly trust anyone from the FBI after the debacle with our WitSec marshal and the resulting attempts on our lives over the years, but because we'd met him though Mason first, I was more tolerant of his FBI associations.

Gabe had worked on a few FPA cases

with Damien and I in the past but I hadn't directly interacted with him much since I usually let Damien play nice with the Feds. From what little I'd seen of him he seemed like a competent investigator. Though not exactly the warmest personality.

He reminded me of a strict schoolteacher I had as a kid. Frosty and sharp, like he could cut you just by looking at you while simultaneously critiquing every mistake you'd ever made. Except, unlike the teacher of my past, Agent Long obviously hit the gym a lot more. His chestnut brown hair was slicked back, and a pair of sharp glasses sat on his nose with such symmetrical balance I wondered if he glued them there.

The man sat at the chair near my desk, fingers steepled in front of him like he was waiting for me to turn in a late homework assignment.

"Damien, I wasn't expecting your brother to join us."

Damien guided me over to my desk, making sure my crutch didn't knock against any stray chair legs, before claiming his own seat behind his desk.

"This involves him as well as me. More so, since he was the one attacked. He should hear whatever you have to report."

Agent Long frowned, but before he could say anything, he was interrupted by the second agent sitting in the last chair positioned in front of Damien's desk.

"Makes sense to me. We need all the mind power we can get on this case, and I've seen some of the cases you and your brother have helped us with before. I'm sure you'll be an invaluable asset."

I shifted in my seat, hiding my grimace as I struggled to find a comfortable position for my leg.

The man was a stranger to me, and even Damien didn't seem to recognize him since he didn't address the man by name.

Such quick praise from someone unfamiliar made me uncomfortable, but I bit my tongue before I said something regrettable. I'd always been a suspicious person. It was how Damien and I stayed alive so long. However, there was a difference between healthy caution and inventing enemies out of thin air.

Rather than confront the stranger, I kept my tone as neutral as possible.

"Sorry, I don't think we've met. What's

your name?”

Luckily, the man didn't seem insulted by my question. He merely laughed in a way that was clearly directed at himself.

“Right. Sorry. We haven't actually met. You and your brother have been mentioned so many times around the office, I feel like I already know you. I'm Blake Adder. I'm in charge of the CAP case.”

Only a few inches of space divided Damien's desk from my own, so I didn't have to lean far in order to speak directly to him. “CAP case?”

“Remember that case I told you about before, where someone's been going around castrating pedophiles? The FBI has determined that it's definitely the work of an organized group and have started calling them the Castration Anti-Pedophiles group. CAP.”

Agent Adder's laughter rang out again. “Yeah, I definitely drew the short straw when it came to assignments. Most people in the agency don't want me to succeed, not even me. I mean, who would want to stop people that are punishing pedophiles? Anyway, my whole assignment is basically just for show, so that we can legally say we're doing our job."

The sound of a throat clearing cut off Agent Adder's raucous laughter.

Agent Long never actually looked at his companion. All of his focus remained fixed on adjusting his lambskin gloves, but his attention was clearly pointed in Agent Adder's direction. "Enough. Get on with it. We don't have all day to sit around."

I shifted again, tipping my leg to a new angle. My tumble off the weight bench earlier was catching up with me, and a new ache had started in my knee. "Since you're here, I'm guessing that the missing children I was looking for are somehow related to your CAP group?"

"Well, sort of."

Agent Adder pulled out a thin laptop from his briefcase and placed it on Damien's desk, though he angled it so I could see the screen as well. He looked at Agent Long and gestured at the laptop.

"Do you want to..."

Agent Long stared at him and said nothing.

"Right, I'll just..." He turned on the screen to show pictures of a kitchen that looked like it hadn't been remodeled since the sixties with an alarming amount of blood staining the floor.

"Agent Long has been looking into Smith Harper, the man who worked for two of the adoption agencies in question. It actually wasn't that hard to track him down, however, when we sent agents to his address, we found him passed out on the floor. Castrated. He's the CAP group's latest victim. So far as we know the group hasn't killed anyone, but apparently something went wrong and they came close this time. In the process of removing... certain parts of Mr. Harper's anatomy, the attackers also cauterized the wound with some form of crude heat or something, so that wasn't what put him at risk, really. Anyway, before authorities could arrive, Harper must have tried to get to his feet and dispose of evidence on his computer. We found the smashed computer pieces—ironically the fool missed the hard drive entirely so we found a bunch of incriminating evidence anyway, plus there was a zip drive filled with information on this guy's activities just sitting there on a side table—but anyway, in the process of trying to get loose from where he'd been handcuffed to a table, Harper busted up one of the table legs and somehow managed to fall and impale himself on it. If our agents hadn't arrived when they did, he probably would have bled out and died."

I sucked in air through my teeth as my leg gave a painful twinge. Both the agents and my brother looked at me, and I schooled my face into a thoughtful expression. "So, we were right. The missing kids were taken to supply some sort of pedophile ring."

"Hold on," Damien cut me off, though he gave me a soft look that said he wasn't trying to argue. "How do we know for certain that this was the work of your CAP group? Just being castrated isn't enough to make that assumption. There are certainly other instances of castration that aren't related to them. A jealous lover. An act of revenge. Or even..." Damien's eyes flickered to me. "Or even a mafia hit could all account for this kind of attack."

I could tell just from Damien's expression that the same memories played behind both our eyes. It was a familiar and well-traveled path of thought.

Even after so many years, it was still hard to ignore the memories of our parents, but I pushed their image out of my mind to focus on the current dilemma.

"It would be an odd coincidence. A suspect in a case involving a pedophile ring, getting attacked in the same way as a vigilante group that targets pedophiles."

"True," Damien agreed. "But we've chased that rabbit down a tunnel of assumptions before, and it doesn't lead anywhere good."

"Well, in this case," Agent Adder said as he opened a different file on his computer. "The CAP group always leaves behind some obvious evidence of their victim's crimes. In this case, we've got a terabyte's worth of child pornography that Smith Harper was distributing."

"So if—" I leaned a little too far sideways and my leg bumped the desk. The grunt of pain that wanted to leave my lips stayed locked behind my teeth, but I couldn't stop myself from visibly flinching.

Agent Long grumbled as he abruptly stood from his chair. "Oh, for the love of..."

Storming over to me, he grabbed my chair and forcibly spun me around. I was by no means a small person, so the sudden manhandling caught me off guard. I didn't even protest as he repositioned me to sit parallel to my desk, then dragged his own chair over and used it to prop up my injured leg.

"You're going to end up back in the hospital if you keep neglecting yourself like that."

I stared up at him, speechless, with my eyes nearly popping out of my head.

He merely raised one perfectly manicured eyebrow. "What? I was a medic in the army. I know what a person looks like when they're hiding pain. You seem like the kind of patient I would have hated to have back then. Ignoring advice. Pushing yourself too fast. Ridiculous. Now, sit still and behave so we can get on with the case."

Since his chair was now being used, Agent Long chose to stand off to the side of the room with his arms crossed.

I couldn't help the grin that spread over my face. Maybe this man wasn't as boring as he seemed.

"I was right. You do remind me of my old schoolteacher."

"You mean Mr. Shaw?" Damien asked,

though he was already giving Agent Long a considering gaze. "I had that guy for eighth-grade algebra. At least half of the students broke down crying during his class that year. Now that you mention it, I do see the resemblance."

Agent Long sniffed and adjusted his already straight glasses. "Ridiculousness runs in your family, I see. Don't know why I bothered. Let this idiot lose his leg for all I care. Adder, hurry up and show them the video so we can get out of here."

"Video?" I perked up in my chair but made sure to keep my leg stationary when Agent Long scowled at me again.

Agent Adder pulled up a video on his laptop that seemed to be a black and white recording from a security camera.

"Right before he was attacked, Smith Harper visited another hospital. We acquired the security footage from the hospital to see if he met with anyone or did anything suspicious. So far, we haven't found anything. All he did was pick up a few brochures for volunteer opportunities and then leave. We were hoping you might notice something that we didn't, since you have the most experience with this case."

The video played, showing a view of the front doors of a hospital where dozens of people were constantly going in and out. The agents had to point out which man was Smith Harper. I'd never seen him before, and even Damien only knew the man by name, not by face. He was entirely unremarkable. The kind of man no one would look at twice if they passed him on the street. Even knowing who I was looking for, he was still hard to keep track of among the hospital rush. Each time the video switched to the view from a new camera, we had to stop a moment and find our target again.

It was like a real-life version of "Where's Waldo" but much less interesting and with much higher stakes.

Just as the agents had described, Smith Harper did nothing suspicious. He barely spent more than a few minutes in the hospital. He loitered in the lobby as he browsed the rack of brochures for volunteer opportunities, then stepped over to the front desk and spoke with the receptionist. From the way he gestured at a few of the brochures in his hand, he seemed to be asking questions about the volunteer work, which the receptionist was happy to talk about.

Then he left. The entire video was less than ten minutes long, and entirely useless for our investigation.

Agent Adder switched off the screen. "This was the last sighting of Mr. Harper before he was attacked. Only about two hours passed between the time of this video and when our agents arrived at his house to find him bleeding out on the floor, so he must have been attacked during that window. Though, as usual, the CAP group was careful not to leave any evidence of their break in."

The agent started to close the laptop, but Damien stopped him. My brother and I shared a look, nodding at each other, before I leaned back in my chair to let him explain.

"This video has been edited," Damien said as he hit the play button.

We all watched as the security cameras once again showed Smith Harper stepping through the front doors into the hospital lobby.

Agent Long stepped closer so he loomed over both desks. His shadow cast a dark pall over the video.

"Nothing's been altered. I handled this

recording myself, and I would never allow a piece of evidence to be tampered with."

I snorted.

Damien cut me a quick look, begging me to stay silent.

"No one is saying that it's been tampered with. But the video has been edited to start at the moment Smith Harper shows up at the hospital. Where's the rest? Has anyone checked the cameras during the time before his arrival?"

One would think we had asked the FBI to hand over nuclear launch codes. Neither of the agents had the uncut footage with them, and when they called their agency they were put through an ungodly game of phone tag as they tried to find the right person who could authorize their request.

Not for the first time, I was glad Damien and I had decided to become private investigators, rather than pursuing jobs with official law enforcement. There was far too much red tape for my liking. The paperwork alone would drive me insane.

Half an hour later, the agents finally managed to procure the original footage.

It took a few minutes of searching to find the right time frame, but eventually we were looking at the hospital's front lobby minutes before Smith Harper's arrival.

Damien pointed at the screen. "Can you zoom in on the brochure display? That's where Harper went first. It may be important."

Agent Adder did as Damien asked, though the footage became more grainy the more he zoomed in. Even hospitals weren't able to afford high quality cameras, it seemed.

Damien and I saw what we were looking for at the same time and ordered Agent Adder to stop the video.

"Right there." Damien tapped the screen with the tip of a pen. "Most people who visit the brochure display only look for a moment before moving on, but this man stayed there for a few minutes." Hitting the video controls, he rewound the video back a few seconds. "And right here. He pulls out several brochures only to immediately return them. However, with this one, it looks like he puts back two pieces of paper instead of just one. I'm almost positive that's the same brochure Harper takes with him a few minutes later."

Agent Long braced his hands on the desk to lean closer to the screen and readjusted his glasses for a better view. "So, it was a hand off. This man leaves something behind, and Mr. Harper picks it up without anyone realizing what's happened. Information. Payment. It could be anything. Is there a better angle where we can see this man's face?"

The mysterious man on the video must have been aware of the hospital's security, for he either kept his back to the camera or made sure to walk on the other side of someone.

He was careful, but not careful enough. We had to switch to a recording from a different camera, but just outside the doors we managed to finally get a brief look at the man's face.

Damien immediately slammed the laptop shut, as though afraid the man would somehow see us through the recording.

I said nothing, but reached out and grabbed my brother's arm as my heart raced inside my chest.

Agent Adder rescued his laptop from Damien's desk and looked like he was about to protest the mistreatment of his equipment when Agent Long cut him off.

"What's wrong? Do you two recognize him?"

I couldn't speak. The man's voice was screaming in my ears, followed by the sound of a gunshot and visions of my parents on the floor, blood surrounding them.

Thankfully, Damien had my back. He looked just as disturbed as I felt, but he at least managed to find his voice.

"That's Lorenz Mariano."

"The brother-in-law of David Russo, the New Jersey Mafia Boss? Are you sure?" Agent Adder arched an eyebrow.

My fist hit my desk so hard it rattled the wood and popped open one of the drawers. "We saw Russo kill our parents, and he wasn't alone. His brother-in-law was there too. We've spent years hiding from David Russo and the rest of the Mariano family after your agency failed to protect us. Yes, we're damn sure."

"All right." Agent Long held up his hands in an uncharacteristic show of surrender. "We have to be sure. Our agency will confirm the identification, but I believe you. It looks like this case just got a lot more complicated."

From the moment we saw Lorenz Mariano on the video, Damien had sat practically motionless in his chair. Even when he spoke, he barely seemed to breathe. Yet, all at once his paralysis disappeared. He sprang to his feet so violently that his chair fell to the floor with a crash of wood and metal.

"Is that why they tried to kill Sebastian? If Russo has found us again, then we need to run. Another state. Another country. Anywhere else."

He was already halfway out the office, probably to start packing our essentials right at that moment, when Agent Long grabbed his arm and pulled him back.

"Hold on. Listen. We don't know what's going on for certain, or how it involves Russo and the Mariano family. Right now, you need to stay put so we can protect you. This building has decent security, so you both need to stay inside behind locked doors until we figure out what's going on."

Everyone else was standing. Even Agent Adder had risen to his feet, though he stayed out of the argument. I hated the feeling of being loomed over, and reached for my crutch so I could stand as well.

"You're going to protect us? Just like your agency did last time Russo and his goons were after us? We trusted your so-called *witness protection* and one of your own people sold us out. We only survived because we went into hiding on our own. So, we're sorry if we're not jumping at the chance to trust you this time."

It was a four-way standoff. Two brothers versus two agents. There was no telling how long the silent stare down would have lasted, had the door not suddenly burst open. Like a synchronized unit, all four of us turned to face the interruption.

Newt stood on the threshold with his hair all askew and sweat dripping down his forehead as he gasped for a breath. An angry crimson scrape cut a jagged line along his cheekbone.

"I think someone just tried to kill me."

CHAPTER THIRTEEN

Newt

MY HANDS SHOOK as I held onto the doorframe, my fingers turning white from how hard I gripped the wood. Right after almost being run over, everything had felt numb. However, as I ran the distance to Sebastian's apartment, more and more feelings erupted inside me until I'd become a jittery mess. I probably looked half crazed as I shoved the door open, but I didn't care. All I wanted was to find Sebastian.

As soon as he saw me, Sebastian's face morphed into a look of concern. He held out the arm not gripping his crutch in my direction, inviting me into his embrace.

"Oh my god. Newt, what happened? Come here."

I stumbled over the remaining distance between us and buried myself against his chest. His familiar scent of bergamot and leather calmed my nerves and finally stopped my hands from shaking.

Sebastian couldn't support us both while standing on one leg. So, he sat on the edge of his desk and let his crutch clatter to the floor before wrapping both arms around me.

"Who is this? What's going on? You didn't mention anyone else was involved," someone barked.

I peeked out from the safety of Sebastian's embrace to see two unfamiliar men staring at me with a mix of confusion and suspicion.

Sebastian held me closer. "This is Newt. He's my... boyfriend and has been helping me with my injuries."

We hadn't actually discussed terms yet, and whether or not we were an official couple, so I understood his hesitance over the word "boyfriend". However, I'd used the same term when talking about him to my sister, so it seemed we were both on the same page.

The two unfamiliar men looked very official, dressed in suits and polished shoes. They were definitely government men. One seemed mostly confused, clutching a briefcase in front of him like a shield. The other one, with glasses and perfectly styled hair, glared at me like I'd just pulled a gun on him.

"Civilians shouldn't be involved in this matter," the guy with the glasses and great hair growled.

Damien stepped between us, blocking me from the stern man's suspicious eyes.

"It seems like he's already involved. Newt, you said someone tried to kill you. What happened? Weren't you meeting with your sister?"

Now that I'd calmed down a little, I realized how pathetic I must look to this room full of impressive men. Gathering my nerves and wiping away the terrified tears from my eyes, I tried my best to explain what had happened as calmly as possible.

The unfamiliar men turned out to be FBI agents who had been investigating the recent attempt on Sebastian's life. They had several questions for me, especially the man with glasses.

Unfortunately, I couldn't answer most of them.

"No, I didn't get a license plate. I don't think they had one, but the car looked just like the ones that ran Sebastian off the road. There was even a big swipe down the side like it was in a recent collision."

They weren't convinced by my story. If anything, my lack of helpful details only seemed to annoy them. The one still holding the briefcase in front of his chest even rolled his eyes.

"A black car with dark windows isn't very specific. A similar scratch along the side isn't enough. We can't take that to court."

Sebastian's arm tightened around my waist. "It's still too much of a coincidence to be ignored. This should at least be enough to get a warrant to seize the footage from the traffic cameras outside the restaurant. You were just making big promises about protecting us, but if this is all the work you're willing to put in, then we're probably better off protecting ourselves like we have for the last ten years." Sebastian scoffed.

The man with glasses, apparently named Agent Long, glanced at his companion out of the corner of his eye. "No one is saying that we won't investigate. We're just warning you that there's a good possibility that nothing will come of it."

Although what he said seemed to be intended as a reassurance for Sebastian and Damien, it was also obviously directed at the other agent as well.

The man, introduced as Agent Adder, just shrugged and nodded.

Agent Long seemed to accept this silent agreement, for his gaze turned a little bit warmer as he focused on me and both of the Roth brothers again. "For now, all three of you need to stay here while we look into it. I'll let you know what we find."

"Sounds good," Damien said as he led Sebastian, and by extension me, toward the door. "Sebastian, why don't you go upstairs and rest while I see these agents out. I will also need to give Max and Travis a call to let them know I won't be home anytime soon." Damien frowned, his lips in a tight line.

"I don't need to rest," Sebastian

protested. "A single meeting isn't going to tire me out."

"Well, why don't you take Newt upstairs to rest then. He looks like he's about ready to collapse."

It was a testament to my condition that I wasn't sure if Damien was merely using me as an excuse to get Sebastian to rest, or if I really did look as bad as he described.

Probably both.

Thanks to Sebastian's leg, it took several minutes to guide him up the stairs. Not for the first time, we both cursed whoever decided not to install an elevator in the building. By the time we reached his bedroom, I collapsed onto his bed with a groan of exhaustion.

"Of course this had to be on a day when I met with my sister. Like that wasn't stressful enough on its own."

The bed dipped as Sebastian sat next to me. "How'd lunch with your sister go, by the way? You haven't told me much about her."

I squirmed across the bed until I could lean my head on his chest.

"There's not much to tell. She's a successful lawyer with a movie star fiancé. Her life's a success, so she thinks she knows the secret of life. Apparently, that gives her the right to decide what everyone else needs in order to be as successful as her." I sighed and pressed my face against Sebastian's shirt, inhaling his calming scent. "No. That's not fair. She means well and just wants me to be happy. Unfortunately, that meant using our lunch to set me up on a date."

"Excuse me?"

When I looked up, I was afraid Sebastian would be angry, but instead he only seemed amused.

"Yeah. She brought her fiancé's cousin along. I swear, I didn't know it was supposed to be a date until the end. No one told me."

Sebastian pressed a kiss to the top of my head, spreading warmth all the way down my body to the tips of my toes.

"I'm not upset that you were tricked into a date. So long as you corrected them."

In the chaos of almost being killed, madly running back to Sebastian's apartment, then explaining everything to a pair of FBI agents, I'd forgotten about the cause of my initial anger.

"I did correct them but they didn't believe me. I even showed them your picture and told them we were dating, but they thought I was lying. Apparently, the idea of you and I together is too ridiculous to be believed."

His arm hung around my shoulders, and his thumb drew little circles just above my elbow. It was such a small, absent gesture, I doubted he even knew he was doing it but the action was reassuring nonetheless.

"What's so ridiculous about it? We get along well and have a lot of similar interests."

"We'll, no one expects someone like you to be interested in video games and Disney movies."

"Someone like me?"

Even without looking, I could hear the smile in his voice. Pouting at him, I smacked his chest. "Don't play dumb. You know exactly what I'm talking about, Mister Tall-Dark-and-Handsome. Badass private detectives are supposed to end up with the femme fatale. Not the weird little nerd."

I meant it as a joke, but once the

words were out of my mouth I realized how bitter they tasted.

Sebastian pressed another light kiss to my forehead. "I think you missed a few adjectives." Another kiss on the tip of my nose. "You forgot cute. And funny."

With each new adjective he pressed a kiss to another part of my face.

"Smart. Hardworking. Kind. Great in bed."

"You can't say that last one. We haven't gone all the way yet."

"That can be fixed."

He slipped his hand inside my shirt and ran his fingers lightly over my stomach. His touch made my cock twitch in my pants.

Maybe we should have stayed focused on more serious matters. There were certainly enough to go around. Someone tried to kill me barely an hour ago, and Sebastian had just found out that the man who killed his parents might be after him and Damien again.

However, I didn't want to think about any of that. It would still be waiting for us later, but for now, I just wanted to focus on Sebastian and the sense of intimacy between us.

My clothing quickly found a home on the floor. However, Sebastian's clothing took an extra minute. His pants had to be worked over his cast carefully to keep the cloth from snagging.

Eventually, we were both undressed and I straddled his lap. He leaned against the headboard and held me close, so I practically draped across his chest.

We kissed leisurely, just a unhurried exploration of lips and tongues that built slowly over several minutes. I wrapped my arms around his shoulders as I sat up straight. In this position, with him half slumped against the headboard and me upright, I was the taller one of the two of us for once. It was a heady feeling, looking down at him from such an angle. Our kiss deepened and I nipped at his lower lip while his hands settled on my waist.

"You know," he breathed against my lips as his fingers bit into the flesh of my hips. "Since you're playing the role of a nurse for me, you're going to have to dress the part someday."

I kissed him one last time before pulling back. "Are you asking me to dress up in a sexy nurse costume?"

"Or you could just wear your usual scrubs. Those Pac-Man ones were really cute. I wouldn't mind fucking you while you're wearing those."

Grabbing him by the chin, I tipped his head up so he looked straight into my eyes. "Those are the same scrubs I was wearing when we met. Were you thinking about fucking me even back then?"

"The thought did cross my mind. Especially after you delivered yourself right into my lap." His hands slid down to grip my ass. On the first day we met, I'd fallen on top of him by accident. The memory made heat suffuse my cheeks.

"Is this what you were hoping for back then? For me to pull you into a private room and climb into your lap, just like this?" I flashed what I hoped was a sultry smile at him.

"I certainly wouldn't have minded. But wouldn't you get in trouble for that? There must certainly be rules about having sex in the hospital's back rooms."

I leaned closer until we were almost kissing again. "For you, I'd be willing to take the risk," I breathed the words over his lips.

Sebastian's smirk brushed against my

lips. "Well, Nurse Clary. You've got me here. What do you intend to do with me?"

"Ugh, it's been such a long shift today." I tangled my hands in his dark hair. "I need to let off some steam, and you seem like the perfect tool for that."

"Is that all I am to you? A *tool* for your pleasure?"

He sounded upset, but I could tell from the feeling of his aroused cock nudging against me that he was actually excited by the idea.

Moving my hips, I rubbed myself against him. "I'll take you out for coffee afterward. How about that?"

He gasped from the sudden stimulation and his hands slid down to grip my thighs. "Coffee? I think you'll owe me dinner after this."

"Dinner then." I moved my hips a bit faster, angling myself in just the right way so our arousals rubbed together. "We'll make it a proper date, but only if you successfully get me off."

We had to stop for a moment to retrieve supplies from the nightstand by Sebastian's bed. He rolled a condom into place while I focused on preparing myself. I tried to act like I knew what I was doing, but I honestly couldn't remember the last time I'd gone all the way with someone.

Had it been months?

Years?

Wracking my brain, I realized the last time I let someone inside me was back during college, and that encounter hadn't been particularly memorable.

I tried to act like I knew what I was doing as I slid one finger inside myself while still perched on Sebastian's lap. The angle was awkward and strained my wrist, but it worked. My inner muscles slowly loosened, and I was soon able to add a second, then a third finger. It didn't hurt, but it wasn't pleasant either.

Sebastian grabbed my wrist and stopped the movement of my hand. "Hey. Slow down. You're treating this like a chore you've got to get out of the way."

He squeezed out some lube onto his hand, then replaced my fingers with his own. They stroked inside me slowly, pressing against internal muscles and teasing at my rim.

I gasped and buried my face against his neck as a ripple of pleasure traveled up my spine. He was clearly much better at this than I was.

"You're definitely earning that date," I whispered, a moan following the words from my lips.

"Maybe even a second date?"

I sank my teeth into the muscle of his neck as his fingers brushed over my rim, though I was careful not to bite down too hard.

"Don't push it," I breathed, my chest hitching.

I felt the vibration in his chest as he laughed, but he never stopped carefully working me open. Little by little I softened around him and his fingers reached deeper. I moaned against his shoulder as he hit something inside me that lit up every nerve in my body and stole the strength from my legs. I slumped down on his lap, gasping for air.

I knew that sweet spot existed. I'd found it several times on my own. However, I'd never had a partner locate it so easily.

Most didn't even bother trying.

Seeing my reaction, Sebastian kept tormenting that same spot with his fingers until I was weeping from the over-stimulation.

"There. I think that's enough." He

kissed away the tears from my eyes. "Brace yourself and hold onto me."

I did as he said and gripped his broad shoulders with shaking hands.

His fingers disappeared from inside me, and I instantly missed the invasion, my hole fluttering, but a moment later his hands gripped me tightly around my hips. He repositioned me so the head of his cock pressed against my entrance.

"Deep breath."

His voice tickled against my ear and I could do nothing but comply.

Then, with one short movement, he thrust inside me.

It wasn't as difficult as I remembered. With past partners, the first breach had always been the hardest part to get through, yet this time Sebastian slipped in with only a pleasant amount of resistance. Apparently, his preparation of my body wasn't just more pleasurable than my own attempts, but more effective as well.

I figured Sebastian probably had more experience with sex than me. Not only was he older, but he was more conventionally attractive. He probably had people falling at his feet to sleep with him.

Yet, I couldn't find it in myself to care about our different experience levels when I was the one reaping the benefits at that moment.

He pressed his cock forward until he was sheathed all the way inside me. Then he started moving, pulling out a little before shoving back in. I gasped as each time he struck that inner pleasure spot again and sent my vision spinning.

"Good. So good. Right there. Keep doing that."

While I couldn't stop myself from babbling, Sebastian fell silent. He was entirely focused on each movement, and his dark eyes bore into me with an intense stare.

He sped up, using his hands on my hips to bounce me on his lap. The entire length of his cock slid in and out of me, grinding deep against inner muscles as it dragged against that perfect pleasure spot again and again.

My whole body spasmed in little jolts like I was being electrocuted from the inside. I couldn't see straight through the ecstasy that burned through my veins like fire. Everything blurred together into a gray haze where I barely remembered my own name.

I didn't even realize I'd reached the peak of orgasm until I tipped over it. The sudden height of pleasure slammed into me, and for a moment I feared I had passed out.

Or maybe I'd died.

It would be a pleasant way to die. Much better than being run over by a car.

Sebastian groaned and I felt his cock swell, releasing a warmth into the condom inside me as he found his climax as well. We trembled together until the intensity of our climax finally released us from its clutches. Then we collapsed and lay quietly as we both caught our breath.

Eventually, when my senses returned to me, I'd have to leave the bed and clean us both up. Another bath would definitely be in order. However, just for a moment, I was content to quietly enjoy the little world of safety I'd found within the circle of Sebastian's strong arms.

CHAPTER FOURTEEN

Newt

THE FRANTIC CLICKING of controller buttons filled the room. Sebastian and I sat side by side on his bed, facing the small television on the far wall. Just as he'd predicted, we'd both been banned from leaving the apartment, so we filled our time with games.

We'd just started a game called Cuphead. It was one of my favorites. Sebastian had never played it and expressed interest in giving it a try. I knew he only suggested it in order to spoil me. Platformers were more my preference than his, and this one was particularly difficult.

I watched his character get killed by the crying onion for the dozenth time. His ghost hovered in the air, waiting for me to revive him.

We were still on one of the beginning levels. It was only going to get harder from here, so I predicted a lot of death in our future.

Luckily, Sebastian wasn't the rage-quitting type and took each new death with a sense of humor.

"I'm losing to a vegetable. How are you so good at this?"

I kept pressing buttons, my fingers flying as my gaze stayed locked on the screen. "You need to parry more so you can build up your super-attack quicker."

"What are you two doing?"

I paused the game, my character hanging in midair, and looked over toward the door.

Damien stood in the doorway, confusion on his face as he glanced between Sebastian and the screen.

"Since when do you play video games?"

I stayed silent and let Sebastian answer the question. He still hadn't told his brother about this particular hobby. If he wanted to claim that we were only playing the game because I insisted, that would be fine.

Sebastian shrugged and toyed with his controller even though the game was paused. "They're relaxing. I don't really like the violent ones, but in this one the bullets are magic, and no one actually dies, so it's okay."

Damien nodded along as if he understood, but he still seemed confused. "Why is your character a teacup?"

"I mean..." Sebastian gestured vaguely at the screen. "It is called Cuphead."

"Okay, but that doesn't explain why it's a teacup in the first place." Damien arched a brow.

"I dunno. Why is a teacup fighting vegetables to collect their souls for the devil in order to pay off gambling debts? It's not supposed to make sense. It's just supposed to be fun."

"Wait, this game is about... No, never mind. That's not why I came up here." Damien shook his head as if clearing something from his eyes. He looked at me. "Gabe needs you downstairs. Apparently, someone came knocking on the front door asking for you. He tried to send them away, but they were insistent."

I still wasn't used to referring to Agent Long as Gabe. The man had assigned himself as the Roth brothers' personal bodyguard and was now practically living at the apartment. With me staying there as well, the two-bedroom space was feeling even more cramped than usual.

"Yeah. We'll be right down." I grabbed Sebastian's controller and set both aside before turning off the game. "Tell him we'll be there in a minute."

A minute turned into five before we were able to get Sebastian down the stairs. It was still a frustrating experience, but not as bad as it had been. The first time he had to navigate the stairs with crutches it had taken us over fifteen minutes. Sebastian still couldn't walk without help, but I appreciated any progress.

In the office below, we found an alarming sight. Agent Long had someone pinned to the wall, one hand on their throat while the other pointed a gun directly between their eyes.

"This man was demanding that I let him see you," Agent Long growled.

Frankie peered at me around Agent

Long's shoulder. "Newt. Tell your attack dog to stand down. I come in peace."

I ran over and grabbed Agent Long's arm, trying to get the gun as far away from Frankie as possible. "Please, put the weapon away. That's my roommate."

Agent Long didn't budge. "That doesn't explain what he's doing here."

Both of Frankie's hands were in the air, and his eyes were so wide I could see the whites all the way around the iris.

"I've been dropping by to bring Newt stuff for weeks now."

Agent Long didn't look convinced, but Sebastian grabbed his wrist to forcibly lower the man's gun.

"Hold on for a moment. Newt, is what he said true? Has your roommate been dropping by regularly?" Sebastian asked.

There was no reason for me to be nervous. I hadn't done anything wrong, but with so many people's attention on me demanding answers, I could help but fidget on the spot.

"I mean, yeah, he has. Between work and taking care of you, I haven't had time to go home, so he's been bringing me fresh clothes and stuff like that. I always met him outside. That's why you haven't seen him until now."

"Exactly." With the gun no longer pointed at him, Frankie tried to step forward but Agent Long shoved him back against the wall. "I was worried when I hadn't heard from Newt in a few days. This is normally when I'd stop by, so I wanted to check in on him."

With a heavy sigh, Agent Long finally stored his gun back in its holster. "You're an idiot," he snapped, his brows furrowed.

Now that his life wasn't being threatened, Frankie's attitude immediately returned. His hands planted on his hips, and he glared up at the agent. "Excuse me?"

"Your friend was nearly killed just for associating with Sebastian Roth. If you've been showing up here regularly, you might be a target now as well."

"Woah, hold up. Go back. Someone tried to kill Newt?" Immediately forgetting about Agent Long, Frankie ran to my side and gripped my hands in his own. "Is that true? Why didn't you tell me?" His face mirrored the concern in his voice.

I gripped him back and our cupped hands created a vague yin-yang symbol of contrasts. "The agents said not to talk about it with anyone else. Plus, I didn't want you to worry."

"Well, I'm definitely worried now," Frankie quipped.

Agent Long gripped Frankie by the shoulder and pushed him toward the staircase. "You should be more than just worried. Get upstairs. You're staying here for now until we can figure out if you're in danger."

Frankie had never been the type of person to obey orders, especially not ones delivered so rudely. He immediately spun around and pointed a finger in Agent Long's face. "Oh, no. You can't just boss me around because you have a gun and a badge. I have a job to do. My patients are expecting me."

Agent Long's gray eyes narrowed behind his glasses, but I couldn't tell if he was upset, suspicious, or something else entirely. Every expression on his face was equally sharp, but this one looked different than any other emotion he had shown so far.

"You have no idea the danger you've stumbled into. It's either your job or your life. Take your pick."

With a huff, Frankie tossed a wayward braid back over his shoulder. "Fine. I'll stay here. For now. But I'm going to need some stuff. I didn't come prepared for a sleepover."

"Make a list of what you need, and I'll send some people over to your place to retrieve it. Now get upstairs. There're too many windows in this office. It's not as safe down here."

Between Frankie and I, we were able to get Sebastian back upstairs in a reasonable time. I expected Agent Long to stay downstairs, where he'd spent most of his time since he'd become our bodyguard, but he followed us up to the apartment.

Despite all the times Frankie had come over to bring me things, he'd never actually seen the inside of the apartment. I'd described it to him, but I could tell the sight of the workout equipment and sparring mat taking up most of the living space still caught him by surprise.

"Well, at least there's plenty of equipment for us to use. All right, we may as well get started now."

After living with Frankie for so long, I knew exactly what he was talking about, but the others were obviously confused.

"Get started with what?" Sebastian asked as he set his crutch aside and started to lower himself into a chair.

I caught his arm before he could sit all the way down. He'd only have to get up again.

Frankie clapped his hands together and gestured at the workout equipment spread over the apartment. "Your assessment. I am a physical therapist, after all. Newt wanted my help with your recovery, so you're going to get it. Plus, while I'm walking you through some basic exercises, you can explain to me what exactly is going on and who tried to kill my roommate."

It was a lot to explain and took nearly half an hour to summarize properly. During that time, Frankie did exactly as he promised and guided Sebastian through a specialized workout routine. Most of the exercises featured slow stretching movements and isolations that worked one muscle at a time.

I rarely got to see this side of the treatment process and watched Frankie work with fascination. Frankie was careful to always keep Sebastian's leg supported so the broken bones never had to hold any weight. He also talked a lot. I was used to explaining things to patients in my own job, but this was on a whole different level.

Frankie spoke with a soft neutral tone that soothed stressed nerves but also left no room for argument. He took the time to explain each muscle they focused on, what the exercise was doing for that muscle, and how it related to Sebastian's overall recovery.

By the end, everyone had done a lot of talking, except for Agent Long. The man had taken a seat in a chair at the far side of the room and watched Sebastian's physical therapy session in silence. Yet, he didn't seem bored or uninterested. If anything, he stared at Frankie and Sebastian with more interest than I'd ever seen from him before. What was going through his head, I had no way of knowing, but he was obviously having a lot of thoughts. He kept rubbing his hand over his left arm, tracing invisible stripes along his sleeve like he was counting something.

I'd worked with enough patients to recognize a self-soothing habit when I saw one, but I kept that observation to myself. Agent Long was doing us a favor by staying here to protect everyone. I wasn't going to embarrass him by pointing out a moment of vulnerability.

After forty-five minutes of work, not only had we explained the entire situation to Frankie, but he'd also come up with a treatment plan for Sebastian.

"I'm already seeing a difference in the flexibility between your two legs," Frankie declared as he helped Sebastian into a chair. "You aren't moving the injured leg as much as the uninjured one, so the tendons are getting tight. It'll throw off your balance when you start walking again and will make your recovery even harder. For now, we're going to focus on maintaining flexibility and muscle strength. Once you can start putting some weight on that leg, then we'll also work on bone strength as well."

Sebastian looked tired. He'd exerted himself more in the last forty-five minutes than in the previous three weeks combined. "Don't know why you're bothering to tell me. It's not like I have a choice in the matter. If you're anything like Newt, then you're going to force me to take care of myself whether I want to or not."

When he worked, Frankie always kept his braids tied back in a loose ponytail. Now that their session was over, however, he pulled the tie free and shook out his braids with a sigh of relief. "Damn straight. Someone's got to take care of you, because it sounds like you won't take care of yourself. Mafia hits. Missing kids. Pedophile rings. You certainly like to throw yourself into danger, don't you."

Sebastian's smile held no joy. "Someone's got to. There are too many vulnerable kids out there with no one to protect them. I have the power to help, so of course I'm going to do what I can, even if it means putting myself in danger."

"Well, I approve of your intentions. Protecting people is a noble goal. Although..." Frankie frowned as he looked around the apartment and the lack of living space. "I don't approve of Newt and myself getting dragged into this mess. How long do you think this will take? I don't want to be stuck here forever."

Agent Long spoke up for the first time since stepping into the apartment. "It'll take as long as it takes, and you'll stay where you're safe until I say otherwise."

Still eyeing the apartment, Franking crossed his arms. "Someone's certainly bossy. Although, speaking of staying here, I'm only counting two bedrooms."

The sudden change in topic took me by surprise to the point where I momentarily questioned my own understanding of reality.

Just to be sure, I counted the bedrooms. Yes, there were only two.

"One for Damien and one for Sebastian. I'm sharing with Sebastian obviously. Why does that matter?"

Frankie raised an eyebrow at me, indicating that I was missing something obvious.

"So, I'm sleeping on the couch then?"

The reason for his concern suddenly hit me and I blushed in embarrassment for not recognizing the problem sooner. "Ah, no. Agent Long is sleeping on the couch."

"So where am I supposed to sleep then?"

Once he'd settled down on the couch after his physical therapy session, Sebastian's eyes started to droop. He wasn't asleep yet, but he would be soon.

At first, I doubted he even heard Frankie's question, but he managed to answer with slightly slurred words.

"The couch pulls out into a sofa bed."

Frankie took a horrified step back and glared at Agent Long. "I am not sharing a bed with *blond and dangerous* over there. He's already pulled a gun on me once."

I shrugged, not knowing what else to do. "It's either that or sleeping on the floor. We don't have a lot of options right now. This apartment wasn't meant to hold five people."

Frankie scowled and shook his head in disgust. "Someone obviously didn't think this through before he started barking out orders." He pointed an aggressive finger in Agent Long's direction. "Well? Nothing to add? You were eager to talk when you were bossing me around, but now you've fallen silent. Say something already."

After adjusting his glasses, Agent Long looked up at Frankie and said very decisively, "I'm not blond."

All of Frankie's anger disappeared in the face of such an unexpected statement.

"Excuse me?"

"I'm not blond." Agent Long pointed at his chestnut brown hair, as if we couldn't see it for ourselves. "You called me *blond and dangerous*, but I'm not blond."

Frankie threw his hands in the air, causing his own braided hair to sway wildly around his face. "Well, *light brown and dangerous* doesn't have the same ring to it. Is that really what you're choosing to focus on right now? We get told we have to share a bed, and you're protesting your hair color?"

Sebastian was half asleep on the couch, so I took his arm, helped him stand, and then guided him toward the bedroom. Frankie and the FBI agent were still arguing when I closed the door. I wasn't worried. Frankie could handle himself, and Agent Long was too much of a strict rule follower to shoot someone just for arguing with him.

I left the pair to figure out their sleeping arrangements and instead focused on taking care of my injured boyfriend. Sebastian was asleep the moment his head hit the pillow, and after a moment of debate, I joined him.

It was only noon, but today had already been exhausting, and the coming days weren't going to get any better. I would need all the sleep I could get.

256

CHAPTER FIFTEEN

Sebastian

I WAS DEVELOPING a complicated relationship with hospitals. Over the years, I'd spent too much time in them, both for Damien's injuries and my own. I'd failed to identify the burned John Doe, so the place was a monument of my failure. Plus, several hospitals had also failed to protect the children born under their roofs and handed them over to the hands of pedophiles.

However, a hospital was where I first met Newt, so it wasn't all bad. Apparently, hospitals could produce good memories as well.

I was feeling especially generous toward hospitals when I went in for an appointment and was told by the doctors that my leg was healing faster than expected. It had been nearly six weeks since my high-speed plummet off a bridge. Ever since Frankie had moved into our apartment, he and Newt had dedicated themselves to my recovery. They had nothing else to do, trapped inside under the guise of "protection" just as I was.

Gabe kept Newt, Frankie, and me on strict lockdown. We hadn't even been allowed to step foot outside the apartment in three weeks.

I could almost understand his protective attitude toward myself and Newt. After all, there had been direct attempts on our lives. Gabe's strict regulation of Frankie, however, was more of a mystery. Yes, the man was possibly in danger because of his association with us, but so was Damien. Yet my brother retained some freedom of movement and was still helping the FBI investigate the possible connection between the pedophile ring and David Russo, the Mafia Boss who had killed our parents.

Every time I watched Damien step out the door while I was stuck inside, I felt a little more useless. I was also climbing the walls with claustrophobia. Movies, video games, and physical therapy could only occupy so much of my time, and still left many hours of the day free to wallow in self-pity.

Several times, I'd had to stop myself from snapping at Newt and Frankie and telling them not to coddle me. That wouldn't be fair when they were only trying to help me.

Their efforts were definitely paying off.

After only six weeks, the doctors declared the crack in my femur healed and swapped out my full leg cast for a sturdy boot that only reached to my knee. The broken bones in my lower leg still needed some time to heal, but the boot provided enough support to let me walk without the damn crutch.

When I returned to the front lobby where Newt and Gabe waited, I held out my arms to show off my hands-free standing capability.

"Looks like you and Frankie know what you're doing, Newt. Even the doctors were surprised by how well my leg has healed. In a few weeks, I'll even be able to get this boot off, and then I'll be completely back on my feet again."

Slipping under my arms, Newt wrapped his arms around my waist in a tight hug. "I'm just glad you're feeling better."

Gabe tucked a small book into his inner jacket pocket, which he had apparently been reading while he and Newt waited for me.

"Great. You're done. Now, let's get back. You're too vulnerable here."

We were at the same hospital where Newt worked. I'd expected he would want to stop in and say hello to his co-workers, or at least check with his bosses that he still had a job despite taking off for a month and a half with no warning.

However, there was apparently no time for socializing as Gabe herded us out of the building and directly into his personal car.

People under the FBI's protection did not walk anywhere or take public transport. No, we got chauffeured like a pair of spoiled celebrities.

Damien and Frankie waited for us at the front door of our building when we pulled up.

"So, how'd it go?" Damien asked as he held the door open for me.

I gestured down at my leg. "Not fully recovered yet, but a hell of a lot better." I turned to Frankie. "I haven't really thanked you or Newt. The two of you have put a lot of effort into helping me recover. I know I haven't been the best patient, but I am grateful."

Frankie grinned and lightly punched my shoulder. "Remember that gratitude when I send you my bill. Private therapy like this doesn't come cheap."

Before I could reply, Gabe stepped between us. "Why are you down here? Don't stand in the open door. You're an easy target."

Heaving a sigh, Frankie rolled his eyes and gave me a pathetic look. "Sometimes, I think he forgets which one of us the mafia is actually after."

Gabe said nothing, but his glare spoke volumes.

"All right. All right." Frankie threw his hands up in defeat. "I'm going back inside. Damn. You're worse than my mother, and she wouldn't let me spend the night at a friend's house until I was sixteen."

Once everyone was safely back inside and gathered in our office on the first floor, I finally noticed the addition to our group.

"Agent Adder. Why are you here? Do you have any new information?"

The man placed a protective hand on his briefcase, which sat on my desk. He, and the other agents that occasionally stopped by to check in with Gabe, had been getting more use out of my desk than I had over the last few weeks. Even the office barely felt like mine anymore.

"I might have something," he said as he tapped the briefcase's latch without opening it. "But I'm not sure."

I waited for him to continue, but the man silently looked toward Gabe and Damien, like he was waiting for instructions.

"What? Not gonna tell us?" I looked over at my brother and Gabe, and it clicked. "Oh, you're just not gonna tell me. What? You think I'm some sort of liability. This was my case to begin with and now you're trying to freeze me out."

Agent Adder had apparently gotten so used to me hobbling around on crutches that he was startled when I took a threatening step toward him.

"No, that's not..." He stumbled back, bringing his briefcase with him like he was afraid I'd steal it. "I just don't want to stress you out unnecessarily. This might turn out to be nothing."

"Nothing?" I was practically yelling at this point. "Don't feed me that excuse. We've already got so little to go on, anything is something. You're just trying to keep me away from this case because you think I can't handle it."

Damien slipped between me and Agent Adder. "Sebastian. It's not like that. We want your help with the case, but we also want you to focus on healing. If there's something you can help with, we'll let you know. But let us weed through the unnecessary stuff first. There's no reason for you to get worked up over every dead end."

Off in the corner, Frankie and Newt were whispering together. I didn't think much about this until Newt inserted himself between me and the others.

"Okay. Everyone calm down. How about this, Sebastian? You and I will go upstairs while the others discuss whatever Agent Adder has found. We need to review the information the doctors gave you today and come up with a new recovery plan now that you're on the mend. Afterward, the others can then tell you if Agent Adder's new information has actually resulted in anything."

That sounded exactly the same as not being involved in the case at all, but I couldn't argue. Newt looked so hopeful. It would take a stronger will than mine to say "no" under the full weight of those pleading blue eyes.

As we left the office, I expected Frankie to come as well. After all, as my physical therapist, he was equally involved with my recovery. However, when I noticed he wasn't following us and asked him about it, he just waved me off.

"Nah. I'm gonna stay down here. You guys can handle it on your own without me."

That was a confusing response, but I was too angry to think about it for long.

At least the staircase was easier to navigate without the crutch. I didn't even need Newt's help getting up to the apartment. The boot on my foot required some getting used to in terms of balance, but each step came a little easier.

My irritation over the situation remained, but I didn't feel so blindly angry by the time the apartment door closed behind me. "What do you need to know? The doctors didn't say much, other than to keep doing what you're doing."

Newt giggled, and the light sound instantly lifted my mood. "Oh, I don't actually need to go over anything. That's just what I told the others." He pressed up against me, slipping my coat open one button at a time. "I recognize the type of cast they gave you. It's a pretty good one. Sturdy. Light. Even waterproof."

He was obviously hinting at something, but my mind was still half occupied by the conversation happening directly below us right that moment.

Luckily, Newt was willing to spell things out for me.

"You've been complaining for weeks that you want to take a shower. Now you can, and there's no one else here, so..."

Finally realizing what he meant, I glanced around the empty apartment. A stack of recently folded laundry sat in the corner of the room since there wasn't enough closet space for everyone's clothes. A spreadsheet had been taped to one wall, listing out the designated times for people to use the bathroom. The sofa was pulled out into a bed, and a line of pillows and blankets had been piled in the center to divide Frankie's side from Gabe's.

With five people living in an apartment meant for two, even with Damien spending most of his time with Max and Travis, there was never a moment of privacy. Newt and I hadn't had sex in weeks. It shouldn't have been that big of a deal. I'd gone the first thirty-three years of my life without him. A few weeks of celibacy shouldn't matter, but now that I'd had him, I wanted more.

Maybe I could let the others work on the case without me, at least for a few hours.

After one brief but intense kiss, we ran for the bathroom as quickly as my cast would allow. Our clothes lay scattered over the floor like the trail of breadcrumbs that were supposed to lead Hansel and Gretel home, except I had no intention of going anywhere else. Getting lost in the woods sounded just fine so long as Newt was there with me.

I'd never been more grateful for the extra expense Damien and I had dedicated to refurbishing the bathroom than when I finally stepped under the hot spray of the shower after taking only baths for a month and a half. The wide rain-shower head and gray tile felt like a luxury spa, and the frosted glass created a private ambiance. There was just enough space for two people, with maybe a foot of air between us. I breathed a sigh of relief as I ran my hands through my hair and reveled in the water running over me.

"Finally." I scrubbed shampoo firmly into my scalp and let the shower wash it away. "Not that your assisted bathing wasn't pleasurable, but trying to wash while keeping my leg propped up out of the water was getting old. It's great to be able to just take care of myself."

Wiping the water from my eyes, I looked toward Newt to see him leaning against the wall and watching me with a hungry gaze.

His wet hair hung in his face. The water made it a shade darker than when it was dry so that it almost looked brown. His blue-eyed gaze traveled down my body, following the path of soapsuds as they dripped over my chest and stomach.

"I hope you don't plan on taking care of everything yourself." His fingers followed the path of the soapsuds down my body until he reached my half hard cock. "There are some things I'd still like to help with."

He wrapped his hand around my shaft and slowly started stroking me. It felt good, but I didn't let it go on for very long. We'd done this before. Now that I could stand on my own two feet, I had other ideas.

Grabbing his shoulders, I pressed his back against the wall of the shower and devoured him with a hungry kiss. I was significantly taller than him, but it had never mattered before since I was always sitting or lying down when we had sex. I could finally use my size to its full advantage. Taking control, I pinned Newt's wrists to the wall as I loomed over him.

He gasped at the rougher handling and tipped his head up to give me easier access to his mouth.

The air filled with steam and left streaks of condensation on the glass.

Newt rubbed a leg against me, urging me on without breaking the kiss.

I couldn't take it. After so many weeks of playing it safe and sticking to only tame forms of intimacy, I needed to be more adventurous.

Not giving Newt a chance to protest, I let go of his wrists and instead grabbed under his thighs and lifted him up.

"Sebastian, what are you doing?" he screeched as he clung to my shoulders.

I wrapped his legs around my waist and pressed him against the wall once again so our hips ground together.

"I'm showing you one of my favorite positions. I really like doing it standing up, but with our size difference it would be difficult. So, problem solved."

"Problem not solved." He slapped my chest then clung to me with all four limbs like half an octopus. "You need to be careful. Your leg still isn't fully healed yet."

My lower leg still ached in the cast, but the sweet relief of finally being able to bend my knee again drowned out any pain I felt. The rubber traction on the bottom of the boot even let me stand on the shower's slick tiles without much trouble.

I distracted Newt with pressing little kisses over his cheeks, one for every freckle.

"It's fine. You're light as a feather. I won't break just from this."

He opened his mouth, obviously about to argue some more, so I pressed my mouth to his again.

Our moans echoed off the shower walls as we rutted and ground against each other. My cock throbbed with desire from the teasing stimulation, and I wanted nothing more than to be buried inside him right that moment.

While Newt clung to me with both arms and legs, I was able to free one hand in order to palm his ass and slowly inch my fingers toward his hole. He gasped and accidentally bit my lip when I brushed my fingers over his rim, but the jolt of unexpected pain only excited me even more.

Very carefully, I slid one finger inside him. With only water and soap for lube, I had to go slower than usual. Pushing one finger in and out of him, I waited until I felt his muscles soften and relax before adding a second digit and repeating the process. He squirmed and mewled, but never let go of me or tried to make me stop.

Judging by the arousal standing tall between his legs, he was just as excited by the new position as I was.

Finally, after several minutes of work, he was ready for me. However, as I grabbed more soap to slick up my cock, I realized a problem.

"Shit. We don't have..." Growling in frustration, I tipped my forehead to lean against his. "There aren't any condoms in the shower."

We panted against each other, sucking in humid air as our breaths mixed with the steam of the shower.

Newt twisted a lock of my hair around his finger. "You know, I've seen your medical records. I know you're clean. If you believe me when I say that I am as well, we wouldn't need to use protection."

I gripped him tighter and practically crushed him against the wall. "I believe you. Are you sure?"

He nodded, then blushed and buried his face against my shoulder. "I want..." His voice cracked and he tried again. "I want to feel you with no barriers."

The image his words invoked set my blood boiling inside my veins. "Fuck yes. Just you wait, baby. You're going to feel all of me."

Given the green light, I wasted no time preparing myself. I readjusted my grip on Newt, so my cock lined up easily with his entrance. The head of my shaft rubbed against his rim, teasing him for a moment, but neither of us were patient enough to wait. He moaned and hooked his hands behind my neck to pull me closer. I could barely hear his breathless voice over the sound of the shower as he begged me to hurry up.

It was a demand I was happy to meet.

The new position, with Newt's legs bent upward to wrap around my waist, made him tighter than usual. I groaned as I slowly sank into him. His inner muscles gripped my dick so tight I feared I was hurting him, but he only moaned and begged for more.

Once I was all the way inside, I started with little thrusts, barely pulling out at all before burying myself back inside. Even such a small drag of skin against skin sent shocks of pleasure up my spine.

Newt pleaded with each thrust.

"So. Good. Sebastian. More."

Our mouths locked together in another kiss, and I picked up the pace. With each new thrust, I pulled out a little more until the entire length of my cock was plunging in and out of his eager body.

Newt screamed into the kiss and dug his nails into my skin. It seemed I had found a particularly good spot. Thrusting back in at the same angle, I hit that spot again and he wailed.

It was a fun new game. Hit the target and win a prize.

I drove into him, focusing on every breathy moan and rough grunt he made. His sounds were a map, leading me to the culmination of his pleasure. My own orgasm almost didn't matter, though I could feel it slowly approaching as a coil of desire turned tighter and tighter in my stomach. As long as I could see him fall apart in my arms, I would be satisfied.

He finally fell off the cliff, crying out my name, the sound of it bouncing off the shower walls. I watched with rapt fascination as his blue eyes lost focus and clouded with ecstasy. He clung to me so tightly, wet skin desperately digging into wet skin, and I couldn't help but follow him a moment later. My climax hit me hard and fast, and I buried my face against his hair as I emptied myself inside his clutching walls.

It was a good thing our apartment had a decent water heater, or else the shower would have turned cold by the time I'd calmed down enough to set Newt back on his feet. We were both a little wobbly, still riding the residual adrenaline that flowed through our veins, and we helped balance each other as we finished cleaning up.

Still, I wasn't done. As soon as we stepped out of the shower, I pulled him into another long kiss that stirred my desire all over again. We didn't even bother to dry off before I dragged him to the bedroom for round two.

Finally, I could lay his sweet figure out over the pillows and take him apart properly piece by piece. His nails dug into my back when I thrust inside him again, kneeling over him this time with his legs spread wide to accommodate me.

"No, I can't," he begged even as he pulled me close. "I just came. It's too much."

He kept saying no, kept begging for mercy, but his legs wrapped tight around me and pulled my hips into him even harder. I followed this physical instruction and pounded into him hard and fast, pushing us both toward our second orgasm in only a few minutes. Yet, even as the pleasure overtook me and I heard him cry out again, I knew this still wouldn't be enough to satisfy either of us.

Sometime later, when we finally finished and lay tangled together on the mattress, I looked toward the clock to find that two hours had passed since we first entered the apartment. The sun was starting to sink outside the window, casting everything in a warm amber hue. It brought out the golden tones in Newt's hair, as though some heavenly being had gilded him around the edges.

Our quiet intimacy was disrupted when Newt's stomach growled. Groaning with embarrassment, he hid his face against my chest, but I only laughed.

"Sounds like someone's hungry."

I felt the vibration of words against my skin but couldn't understand what he said.

"What was that, baby?" I grinned.

He raised his head just enough to repeat himself clearly. "It's not my fault.

You wore me out. How many times did we even do it? You're an animal. Take responsibility."

I pressed a kiss to the tip of his nose, happy to comply. "All right. Let me see what we have in the kitchen. You and Frankie have kept this place stocked with all kinds of healthy stuff, but I think we've got a stash of your favorite M&M's as well."

I rose from the bed and grabbed a pair of gray sweatpants that were hanging over the arm of a chair. As I pulled them on, I took a moment to marvel at how easily they slid over my new cast. I could almost forget it was even there.

"Wait," Newt called as I reached for the door. "You should relax. I'll go get us something."

He moved as if he meant to get up, but I shook my head. "Let me do it. You've been catering to me for weeks. Now that I can finally walk, it's my turn."

It took very little convincing for Newt to lie back down. I hesitated for a moment, enjoying the sight of him sprawled among my sheets with the setting sun running golden fingers over his skin.

It was only because of this moment of

hesitation that I noticed an odd sound. Quiet footsteps echoed in the room just beyond the door. In an apartment currently housing five people, footsteps were not uncommon, but what caught my attention was the unfamiliar pattern.

My brother's footsteps I could recognize even in the dark. Gabe and Frankie I was less familiar with, but the pattern didn't seem to match what I'd observed of them so far.

Gabe stalked silently, but with purpose, like an arrow being shot from one place to another.

Frankie was louder, but always careful, as though he were dancing his way through life.

These footsteps were neither.

"Hello," I called. My hand still rested on the doorknob. "Did you guys finish your meeting already? Finally going to tell me what you found?"

Maybe I was wrong about the footsteps. I'd only known Gabe and Frankie a few weeks, after all.

I waited for a reply, desperately hoping to hear a familiar voice and prove I was just being paranoid.

No one spoke, but the footsteps picked

up their pace. They grew softer and farther away. Then the door leading out of the apartment closed with a barely audible sound of squeaky hinges.

I opened the bedroom door, intent on going after whoever had been inside the apartment, but the minute I turned the handle, I heard an ominous metallic click.

"Fuck!"

Diving from the door, I grabbed Newt and rolled us both to the floor on the other side of the bed.

Then the whole world exploded around us.

We were thrown against the wall. My vision went black, but I was still conscious. A high-pitched whine screamed in my ears. Everything hurt, and yet was strangely numb at the same time.

I couldn't breathe.

None of that mattered. I could still feel Newt's weight in my arms. He seemed to be in one piece.

But was he alive?

This thought spurred me into motion. I opened my eyes and struggled to see through blurry vision. Newt's face greeted me. Bright red blood trickled down his forehead, nearly the same color as his hair. His eyes were closed.

My first instinct was to shake him and demand a response. I so desperately wanted to hear his voice, but I stopped myself at the last moment. If he was injured, too much movement would make it worse.

His chest rose with a shallow breath.

He was alive.

I could handle anything else so long as he was alive.

What the fuck had happened?

As I rose up from the floor into a sitting position, Newt cradled in my arms, my shoulder screamed with pain. A splinter of wood several inches long stuck out of my flesh. I couldn't pull it out without letting go of Newt. The stake would have to stay in place for now.

Some sort of explosive. That's what my mind told me. There had been some sort of explosive on the other side of the door, likely triggered when I turned the handle.

My head hit something solid when I sat up. Everything was darker than it should have been. I felt along the solid surface hovering over us and realized I was looking at the underside of my bed frame.

When the explosive went off, the bed had been thrown across the room. It probably would have killed us, but luck was on our side. The frame had wedged perfectly in the corner, creating a little pocket of safe space.

It would have been so much easier to lie there and just wait for rescue. Surely, Damien was already looking for me. I couldn't see anything outside our protected corner beneath the bed frame, and had no way of knowing what state the apartment was in. Waiting for rescue would probably be safer, and I was so tired. All I wanted to do was lie there and continue holding Newt until everything was safe again.

Except, it was getting hard to breathe.

The air was too thick, and the taste of ash lingered on my tongue.

I let go of Newt just long enough to peer around the damaged bed frame.

What had once been the wall of my bedroom was now a burning hole of wood and plaster. Fire licked every surface it could find, rapidly climbing higher until it touched the ceiling. There was barely any floor left. Our apartment was practically a crater. Even as I watched, a few more floorboards crumbled under the flames, and a half-destroyed chair fell into the burning pit.

More and more thick smoke filled the room. My vision blurred and each breath came a little harder than the one before. Behind me, I heard Newt cough, a deep raspy hacking that made my lungs hurt just from the sound.

If we didn't escape soon, either the smoke or the fire would kill us. Even if rescue was on its way, we wouldn't survive long enough for them to get here.

We needed to get out on our own.

"Come on, Newt," I said to the unconscious man as I lifted him into my arms. "We're getting out of here."

I shoved the remains of the bed frame aside and stumbled to my feet.

Maybe, if I sprinted, I could make it to the staircase without getting too burned by the fire.

That plan was immediately killed when I took a few unsteady steps and one of the floorboards collapsed under my foot. I stumbled back until I hit the far wall. Fire had eaten away at the building's supports. We were practically standing on a pile of matchsticks. There was no way we'd make it to the stairs, assuming they even still existed.

It was a miracle this portion of the apartment was still standing at all.

There was nowhere to go.

More smoke blew into my face, filling my nose and mouth immediately. I coughed so harshly that I nearly dropped Newt.

No, there had to be a solution. We were still alive. So long as we were alive, there was hope.

The window. It was only a few feet away, and the floor around it still looked stable.

I shuffled my way over, stepping carefully.

The building groaned around me, and the fire raged even harder. The skin along my arm blistered from the heat. I tucked Newt closer to protect him from the flames, but there was no escaping the smoke that choked us both with every breath.

I reached the window, grateful to find that the glass had already shattered so I wouldn't have to break it. There were no stairs or fire escape on this part of the building. Only a two story drop between me and the hard concrete below.

More floorboards collapsed, dangerously close to my feet. The whole apartment would soon cave in. I could hear the wood and metal crying out as the flames devoured the room.

I had no choice.

Taking a strong hold on Newt and bracing one foot on the windowsill, I jumped.

CHAPTER SIXTEEN

Newt

I AWOKE TO the sound of endless beeping. I was so tired, all I wanted to do was go back to sleep, but the beeping wouldn't stop. It was driving me mad. Although my eyelids felt like they each weighed twenty pounds, I eventually opened them just to see what was making that sound and how I could shut it up.

The sight that greeted me was a familiar one. White walls and white bed sheets draped over a small bed with railings on either side. It'd seen so many hospital rooms over the course of my career, but never from this side of things.

I was no longer the paramedic bringing someone in on a gurney, or the nurse standing bedside. This time, I was the patient.

What the hell happened?

I didn't normally curse, but those words ricocheted around my skull so hard I visibly flinched.

In the seat next to my bed, Frankie jolted out of the doze he seemed to have fallen into.

Maybe my question hadn't stayed contained inside my head like I thought. I didn't remember using my vocal cords, but either I'd spoken out loud or Frankie had coincidentally woken up at that exact same moment.

"Newt. You're awake." Frankie practically fell out of the chair he was sitting in when he rushed to my side. "How do you feel?"

"Tired. Dizzy." I coughed and pain shot through my lungs. "My chest hurts. Frankie, what happened? Why am I here?"

He fussed, tutting as he carefully used his hands to smooth out the thin blanket covering me. "What do you remember?"

I shooed his hands away and pushed

the blanket down in order to sit up properly. "Sebastian and I were alone. We..." I recalled our moment in the shower, and the several moments we shared afterward. My face burned hot and my headache throbbed.

Frankie didn't need to hear about any of that.

"We were alone in the apartment. Sebastian heard someone and called out to them, but they didn't answer. Then he grabbed me off the bed and..."

I remembered hitting the floor and feeling annoyed when I smacked my head. Then there was nothing. My memory just went black.

"Sebastian heard someone in the apartment?"

I looked up, startled by the unexpected voice, and found Damien standing in the doorway staring at me with the most serious expression I'd ever seen.

I nodded, but quickly stopped when the room spun. "Um, yeah. He thought it was one of you guys, but when he called out to them, they left. Then he opened the door and..."

The smell of smoke assaulted my nose, and I looked around expecting to see something on fire. "I don't know what happened."

Damien looked like he was about to say something, but at that moment a doctor and several nurses bustled into the room.

I recognized them. I'd worked with all of them in the past. They were good people, but at that moment I didn't have any patience for them as they took my vitals, asked how I was feeling, and told me information I already knew.

I had a concussion. That was no surprise.

A deep cut on my head needed stitches. Even more obvious than the concussion.

My lungs had smoke damage. This was a little odd, but not unexpected. I could tell there was something wrong with my lungs every time I took a breath.

None of this told me how the injuries happened, and none of my fellow coworkers seemed inclined to tell me.

Finally, after an extensive examination, I was left alone with Damien and Frankie to demand answers.

The pair looked at each other, seemingly daring the other to speak first.

Eventually, Damien sat by my bed and leaned forward so his elbows rested on his knees in a defeated position.

"Some sort of explosion went off in the apartment. We don't know the cause yet, but I doubt it was accidental. The entire apartment was destroyed. Those of us who were downstairs at the time are fine, but you and Sebastian barely survived. He..."

Damien's voice cracked and I was startled to see tears drip from the man's eyes.

"Sebastian. What happened to him?"

A new thought occurred to me.

What was Damien doing here with me?

If Sebastian was hurt, Damien would want to be with his brother.

Unless...

I couldn't breathe.

"He's not... Damien, tell me Sebastian is alive." My heart thumped beneath my breast and my monitor went wild.

Breathing deeply through his nose, Damien managed to find some composure. "He's alive, but he's in surgery right now. In order to get the two of you out of the apartment, he had to jump out the window. His leg couldn't take the impact. It re-broke worse than before. The doctors are trying to fix it right now, but... He may not be able to walk again."

Before I knew what I was doing, I'd thrown my blanket aside and was halfway on my feet.

"Absolutely not. He can't... I won't let that happen."

"Woah, Newt." Frankie grabbed my shoulders and forced me back onto the bed. "Calm down. What are you going to do, storm the operation room and perform the surgery yourself? The doctors are doing their best to fix his leg, and then afterward you and I will make sure he recovers. All right?"

The surge of adrenaline drained me, and I collapsed back against the thin hospital pillows. "Fine. You're right. I just..." I pressed my hands against my eyes, trying to hold my tears at bay. "It's not fair. He was finally getting back on his feet. Do you know when he's getting out of surgery?"

"It should be soon," Damien said, right before Gabe stepped into the room distracting him.

"I've set security around the building.

This room should at least be safe, so we'll have the doctors bring Sebastian here once they're done."

Damien gave an absent nod as he stood and casually wiped the wrinkles from his clothes. "Safe. Right."

With no warning, he suddenly lunged forward and punched Gabe across the face. The force of the blow sent the FBI agent slamming into the wall.

Damien loomed over Gabe and grabbed the other man's lapel like he meant to punch him again.

"This room is safe? Just like the apartment was supposed to be safe? This is the second time your agency has promised to protect us and failed. Someone got into the apartment and planted an explosive. How were they able to do that when you were supposedly protecting the place?"

Pulling out a handkerchief from his pocket, Gabe wiped the blood from his split lip. "Supposedly? You think I was lying to you?"

Damien's knuckles cracked when his fists clenched. "One of your people betrayed us. It's the only explanation. God, this is just like last time. Nothing has changed. Russo still has spies in your agency."

Gabe eyed Damien's hands warily, ready to dodge another punch, and wisely didn't try to come any closer.

"We don't know for certain that David Russo is involved."

Although Damien stood with his back to me, I could still tell he rolled his eyes just from the sound of his voice. "After what we just discovered. Of course he's involved."

Not wanting to disrupt the argument, I leaned over to Frankie. "What did they discover?"

Frankie kept his voice to a whisper as he also cautiously watched the two arguing men. "Right before everything... blew up. Agent Adder brought some new information. The FBI has been looking into the adoption agencies that we know kids have disappeared from. They found donations to those agencies made by companies that are suspected fronts for David Russo and the Mariano family."

"So, this Mafia Boss guy is paying off the agencies to supply kids to his pedophile ring?"

"Looks that way." Frankie shrugged.

"At least, that's what it seemed like when I was eavesdropping on their meeting."

While we spoke, the argument between Damien and Gabe became more heated until Frankie had to intervene. Technically, Gabe never yelled, but he did seem twitchy and on edge compared to his usual stern appearance.

Damien, however, was obviously struggling to control himself. He excused himself from the room by claiming he was going to check on Sebastian's situation.

I groaned and lay back against the pillows, pulling a blanket over my face to block out the world. It was too much. I wanted to go back to the moment right before the explosion, when everything had been looking up.

That had only been a few hours ago.

How could so much change so quickly?

Gabe eventually also left the room, though he stayed just outside the door to keep watch over things. If there was a traitor among the FBI, which was looking more and more likely, I doubted Gabe was involved. He'd literally lived with us for weeks. If he wanted to harm us, he wouldn't have had to go so far as blowing up the apartment. He could have simply shot us in our sleep.

It was a morbid thought. During my time as a nurse and a paramedic, I'd faced death and injury almost every day, but never my own. Before this whole incident, the closest I'd ever come to mortal danger was when I fell out of a tree as a kid because I wanted to befriend the squirrels that lived in its branches.

That was a much happier thought than worrying over Sebastian's surgery. I refused to acknowledge the doctor's concerns. Sebastian would walk again. Even if I had to spend the next several years personally nursing him back to health, he was going to walk again. Then, we'd go to a park and feed the squirrels, and I'd tell him about the time I climbed to the top of a tall tree because I wanted to be a Disney princess. Every Disney princess has an animal companion they can talk to, so I thought the squirrels could be mine.

He would definitely find the story funny.

When Frankie and I were the only ones left in the room, we passed the time playing cards. With only two people, the games we could play were limited, but it kept us occupied.

I'd just won my third hand of go-fish when someone new walked through the door. There was barely enough time for me to recognize my sister before she rushed over to me, grabbing me in a hug and knocking the cards to the floor.

"Newton, oh my God," she said as she squeezed me. "I got a call from the hospital saying you were in some sort of accident. What happened?"

Accident?

Really?

Was that what the hospital was calling it?

"Um, hey, Rosalind." I awkwardly patted her back. Our lunch meeting hadn't ended on a positive note, and I had no idea where the two of us stood with each other. "I'm okay. Just a bit of a concussion which should clear up."

She held me out at arm's length to get a better look at me, eyeing me up and down. "Okay? You're black and blue all over."

"It's not that bad."

Maybe it was. There hadn't been a chance for me to look in a mirror yet, but no matter how bad I looked, Sebastian must be in a worse state. It felt selfish to complain about a few bumps and bruises.

My sister finally noticed Frankie sitting beside me and held out her hand like it was a business meeting.

"Hi, I'm Rosalind Clary. You must be Frankie Zolnai, my brother's roommate."

It was an oddly formal introduction, but at least she'd gotten his name right.

Frankie accepted her hand but didn't bother replying as she was already talking again.

"Thanks so much for taking care of my brother. Are you the one who brought him in?"

I shouldn't have been surprised when Damien chose that moment to return. The hospital may as well have installed a revolving door with how often people kept coming and going from my room.

The minute I saw Damien, my sister was immediately forgotten. "Any news?"

Damien's expression was neither happy nor sad, but his hands toyed a pair of sunglasses, betraying the man's agitation. "Yeah. He's out of surgery, though he's still unconscious. They won't know how well it went until he wakes up."

"Can I see him?"

"Yeah. They're bringing him in now." It was only then that Damien noticed my sister. "I'm sorry, who are you?"

"Rosalind Clary. Newton's sister. Who are you?"

I could see Damien mouthing the syllables of my name in confusion. He'd likely never heard my full name before, and even if he had, it was so seldom used that most people forgot the name on my birth certificate wasn't actually Newt.

"Dami—Daz Roth. Bastian's brother. Look, you may need to clear out. We're going to need more space for my brother."

Just as Damien had stumbled over my name, I noticed my sister equally puzzled by Bastian's name as she quietly repeated it under her breath.

As though it had been planned, the hospital staff chose that moment to wheel Sebastian's bed through the door. He was unconscious, lying among a sea of white sheets. His normally healthy complexion looked pale, and there were heavy bags under his eyes along with several places where stitches could be seen on his skin.

The worst, however, was once again his leg. This time, instead of a cast, they had his right leg suspended in full traction. There was also a brace around the ankle and knee of his left leg, but those were barely noticeable in comparison.

He looked horrible, but his chest moved. He was still breathing. That was all I could ask for.

The bed was placed only a few feet from mine, and I rose to go to him, but a hand on my shoulder stopped me.

"Newton, where are you going? You need to stay in bed. And you." She turned back to Damien. "I'm sorry for your brother, but why are you here? Surely the hospital has enough rooms. They can't expect patients to share like this."

The nurse who'd helped bring Sebastian into the room looked between everyone, obviously confused. I felt bad for her. She was being reprimanded by my sister for something she'd been explicitly ordered to do. I'd been caught in the same non-winnable situation many times during my own shifts. It was never fun.

At that moment, however, I didn't care. I just wanted to get to Sebastian's side.

"Rosalind, move. I know you're

confused, but right now my boyfriend is injured, and I don't have the patience to explain."

I didn't wait for her to agree and just shoved her aside. She looked surprised to be so easily moved by me despite her significant height advantage. I was stronger than I looked, and years of assisting patients as both a nurse and a paramedic had made me particularly good at moving people who didn't want to be moved.

There was only a few feet of space between our cots, but my legs were still shaky and I had to catch myself on the edge of Sebastian's bed to keep from falling over.

"Careful," Frankie scolded as he helped me sit on the bed properly.

I hovered my hand over Sebastian's face, too afraid to touch. There were so many little cuts and bruises. Many more than I had, despite living through the same disaster.

The reality of the situation finally hit me. Damien said Sebastian had to jump out the window for us to escape.

Us.

Sebastian had been carrying me when

he jumped. He'd probably protected me from the initial explosion as well, based on the discrepancy between our injuries.

That meant his injuries were partially my fault. If I'd only been conscious, I could have made the jump on my own. Even if I broke my leg, it would have been better than expecting Sebastian to carry my weight.

Tears dripped down my face. A few landed on Sebastian's cheek and I wiped them away before they could soak into his bandages.

"Where's his medical file? I want to see it for myself."

The attending nurse tried to stop me, but I grabbed the clipboard from the pocket at the bottom of the bed.

Everything was spelled out so clearly in black and white. Sebastian's recently healed femur had completely snapped, and the bottom half of his leg was shattered. Several metal pins had been implanted to try and piece the bones back together.

His previously uninjured leg wasn't great either. A hairline fracture in his ankle and torn tendons in his knee would have been hard enough to heal on their own. With the two legs together, Sebastian would certainly not be walking any time soon.

On top of all that, there were other injuries as well. His previously cracked ribs were damaged again, there were burns over his hands and arms, and his lungs showed severe smoke damage.

In fact, the only injury he didn't seem to have was a concussion, the one injury I did have.

Between the two of us, we ran the full gambit of pain.

Frankie carefully pried my hands from the clipboard. "Okay, Newt. I think that's enough for now. You're smudging the ink."

I looked down at what he was talking about and realized I'd been crying all over the medical report and wet drops now stained the page.

"Sorry." I let go of the clipboard, and with a little help, I returned to my own bed. As much as I wanted to hold Sebastian in that moment, his injuries needed to stay isolated and not be jostled around too much.

Damien spoke with the nurse, probably discussing Sebastian's care. I should have paid attention to what they were saying, but I was so tired, I just wanted to sleep. I lay back on my own bed with my head propped up on pillows, but I could already tell sleep would evade me. I couldn't even imagine closing my eyes for a while.

The hospital's firm mattress barely moved when Rosalind sat next to me. "Hey, Newton. That man..."

She trailed off, looking over at Sebastian with a mix of confusion and surprise.

"What about him?" I watched her, trying to figure out what was causing her odd reaction.

Then I thought back on our conversation several weeks ago and it hit me. I couldn't help it. I laughed.

It was not a happy sound and made several people wince.

"Surprised? Yes, I was telling the truth about my boyfriend. You believe me now?"

"Yes, I..." She grabbed my hand. "I'm sorry I didn't before."

I just shrugged. "It doesn't matter now."

"It does," she insisted. "I shouldn't have assumed like that. Um, Bastian, was it? When Bastian is awake, I'd like to meet him."

There was no way Sebastian would want to meet anyone while he was in such a state, but I wasn't about to tell Rosalind that. Instead, I just shrugged and said "Maybe."

I was spared from any further awkward conversation when Gabe stormed back into the room. His eyes immediately locked onto my sister, and with his usual tact he just pointed at her and said, "You. Get out."

"Excuse me?" Rosalind jumped to her feet with an offended flush to her cheeks. "You can't tell me to get out. I'm Newton's sister. I have a right to be here."

Gabe barely paid her a spare glance as he headed for Damien and the nurse. "And I'm the agent in charge of this investigation. Now get out. No extra liabilities are allowed inside this room."

"Investigation?" Rosalind turned to me with concern. "Newton? What's going on? The hospital said it was an accident."

"We're still not sure what happened," I told her, which wasn't technically a lie. We still hadn't figured out who or what exactly caused the explosion. Only that it was deliberate. "For now, maybe it's best if you leave. I'll explain everything later."

That was a direct lie. Even once we had all the answers, I would not be telling her everything, but that assurance was the only way to convince her to leave. I would have felt bad for lying, but part of me was still bitter over her early accusations.

She'd assumed I was lying when I told her about Sebastian the first time. Now, I actually was guilty of the thing she accused me of.

CHAPTER SEVENTEEN

Newt

SEVERAL HOURS PASSED before everything calmed down. Sebastian never woke up during that whole time, though that really didn't surprise me. He'd been given a strong anesthetic and was on some pretty heavy pain drugs.

Still, I wished I could speak to him, even for a moment just to assure myself that he was okay.

No, not okay.

With that many injuries, I couldn't say he was okay. But I at least wanted to know that the person I cared about still resided behind his eyes, and that this whole experience hadn't changed him mentally.

Mostly, I just wanted him to tell me that it wasn't my fault and that he didn't blame me for his injuries.

Eventually, it was decided that Sebastian and I needed to be left alone to rest, so Damien and Gabe took their conversation to another room. Frankie had intended to stay with me, but I asked him to go with the others.

Not only did I need a few moments to myself, but I trusted Frankie to tell me the truth. So, I needed him to be involved in the investigation as much as possible, otherwise I feared I'd be kept entirely out of the loop.

So, that was how I ended up lying on my bed alone with the lights turned down low, counting the rhythmic beeping of the machines monitoring Sebastian's health.

I was out of tears, though the urge to cry remained. The logical part of my brain said that it was probably a sign of dehydration, but it was easier to think that I'd simply used them all up.

Surely there had to be a limited number of tears a person could shed.

Why did people cry anyway?

From a biological standpoint, it made no sense. When a person was distressed, unnecessarily wasting water and vital nutrients seemed counterproductive to human survival.

The door to the room quietly opened. I didn't bother looking away from my staring contest with the ceiling, assuming it was either Frankie or Damien coming to check on me. Or maybe even my sister. So many people had come and gone through the door today that I'd stopped keeping track.

The person went over to Sebastian's bedside, so I assumed it was Damien, but the footsteps were too light. At first, I dismissed this observation as paranoid, until I realized the sound of the person's shoes on the floor didn't sound right. The shoe had too much of a heel to be Damien. The man was already over six feet. He didn't need to make himself taller.

As I looked over at Sebastian, the room was dark, but the curtains were open. Early morning light gave me a clear view at the woman standing over Sebastian.

It was Miss Constella, the hospital's administrator. The square glasses and tight bun she always wore were easily recognizable.

"Administrator Constella, what are you doing here?"

She flinched, but quickly calmed herself as she turned to look at me. "Nurse Clary. Forgive me. I thought you were asleep."

I shrugged and sat up, pulling the blanket away so my legs weren't tangled. "It's hard to sleep right now. So, what are you doing?"

"Oh," she gestured back toward Sebastian. "Just administering his medication. We're short staffed today, so I'm helping out where I can."

I laughed as though we were merely chatting in the break room. "When are we not short staffed?"

Even as I said it, my eyes zeroed in on her hands. Her gesture had been strange. The way her body was angled put her right side closer to Sebastian, but she'd gestured toward him with her left hand.

That's when I noticed the syringe held in her right hand.

"What's that?" I nodded toward the syringe while at the same time letting one leg dangle off my bed so my bare foot touched the cold floor.

She didn't raise the syringe to give me a better look, but she also didn't try to hide it either. "Just some extra steroids, to help his lungs heal faster. They were pretty badly damaged from the smoke."

I nodded, keeping my eye on the syringe. "They just administered his meds an hour ago. I'm surprised the doctors are prescribing more. He's already being given a high dose of corticosteroids. Are his injuries worse than we thought?"

One of the things I found most annoying when I'd been studying to become a nurse was the fact that so many medications looked the same. Pills were fine, but liquid medication was almost all clear. As a visual learner, it had made memorizing the different medications very difficult. However, after many hours of work I'd finally managed it.

Now, these seemingly similar medications no longer looked the same. Slight differences in the clarity and viscosity of each liquid were nearly as telling as the name on the label.

Looking at the syringe now, I didn't know exactly what it held, but the liquid inside was definitely too thin to be corticosteroids like Administrator

Constella claimed.

Our eyes met.

We both moved at the same time. She lunged for Sebastian while I dove at her.

Sometimes being small had advantages. I could move quickly in tight spaces.

I grabbed her arm when the syringe was only inches from Sebastian's chest. The two of us tumbled to the floor together. I landed on my back in the space between the beds with Administrator Constella's weight on top of me.

She still held the syringe. Realizing her plan had failed, she changed tactics and plunged the syringe down toward me instead. I caught her wrist before the needle could touch me. We fought for control of the syringe, but the position didn't give me much leverage. I could only push against her with my arms while she bore down on me with all her weight.

Slowly, my strength failed, and the needle inched closer.

"Crazy bitch," I spat through clenched teeth. My legs flailed. I accidentally kicked one of the beds, but I barely noticed the new pain in my foot.

"It's your fault," she said as she pushed the syringe closer. "You shouldn't have interfered."

"And you shouldn't have tried to kill my boyfriend."

I slammed my head forward, knocking my skull right into her nose. It always worked in movies.

While the move did have the desired result, Administrator Constella's nose gushed blood and distracted her long enough for me to grab the syringe, there were unforeseen consequences.

Slamming my head into someone else injured me as well.

My vision spun and pain blossomed all along my skull. This was definitely not helping my concussion, but even though I couldn't see straight, I could feel the cool cylinder of the syringe in my hand.

I'd at least managed that much. Now I just needed to find help.

Holding onto the bed, I rose to my feet and stumbled for the door.

Unfortunately, a broken nose wasn't a fatal injury, and the pain didn't distract Administrator Constella for long. She rushed after me, grabbing my legs to pull me back to the floor.

We grappled over the syringe. Her fingers came dangerously close to clawing out my eyes, so I sank my teeth into the back of her hand.

The taste of blood on my tongue made me draw back. It was much more unpleasant than expected and I nearly lost my grip on the syringe.

"Give up. Whatever they're paying you can't be worth it."

She clocked me with her elbow, and I felt a bruise immediately start to form under my eye.

"A brat like you wouldn't understand." She yanked my hair hard enough to pull my head to the side and managed to get her hands around the syringe.

I kicked her off me, and she crashed against Sebastian's bed. His leg swung in its traction and I flinched, hoping I hadn't made his injuries worse.

"No, I wouldn't understand. I hope I never understand the actions of people like you."

Several orange strands of my hair still hung between her fingers as she glared at me. "Don't be so self-righteous. You'd do the same thing in my position."

I never got to find out what that

position actually was.

Before she could come at me again, she was suddenly yanked backward.

Sometime during our fight, it seemed Sebastian had woken up. Still stuck lying in bed, he leaned as far over the edge of the mattress as he could and locked one arm around Administrator Constella's neck in a stranglehold.

She clawed at his arm but couldn't free herself from the headlock.

Sebastian stared at me with eyes still blurry from his long bout of unconsciousness. It was obvious he'd acted more on instinct than conscious thought.

"Newt, what the hell is going on?"

I looked at him, looked at the syringe in my hand, looked at Administrator Constella, and had no idea where to start explaining.

Then, before I could utter a word, the door opened, and I was met with surprised shouts from both Damien and Gabe.

We must have made a shocking scene.

Me, sprawled over the ground with a syringe clutched in my hand.

Sebastian half falling out of his bed

with his leg still in traction as he kept a stranglehold on a member of the hospital staff.

And Administrator Constella, who had completely forgotten her usually put-together demeanor to spew a series of creative curses as she tried to pry Sebastian's arm off of her.

The image was so absurd, I couldn't help but laugh as relief flooded through me.

Sebastian was awake. I'd protected him from the third attempt on his life, and simultaneously survived the second attempt on my own.

It was someone else's job to take over for a little while.

As I laughed uncontrollably, the room started spinning. Realizing what was about to happen, I flopped down on the cold hospital floor and promptly passed out.

CHAPTER EIGHTEEN

Sebastian

FIFTY PERCENT CHANCE of ever walking again.

That was what the doctors told me.

Fifty.

Fuck.

Two days after my latest brush with death, I lay in my hospital bed, flipping a quarter between my fingers. I didn't even remember where I'd gotten the coin. It had seemingly just appeared in my hand between one moment and the next.

In the chair next to the bed, Damien sat slouched against the wall, head lolling against his shoulder as he snored.

I flipped the coin in the air and caught it before it hit the bed.

Heads: I'd walk again.

Damien shifted in his sleep, grumbling as he struggled to get comfortable in his awkward position, then immediately drifted off again.

My brother had barely slept over the last several days, while I seemed to do nothing but sleep. Even at that moment, I'd only been awake for about an hour and already I felt the need to shut my eyes.

I flipped the coin again.

Tails: I'd never walk again.

We had no idea who to trust and Damien had taken over the job of guarding me himself. However, that couldn't last forever. There were too many people after us. David Russo, and the entire Mariano family by extension. The traitors within the FBI. The perpetrators of the pedophile ring. They were all tied together, and all looking to put me and my brother six feet under.

The coin flipped.

Tails: I'd never walk again.

No one had said it yet, but we would need to disappear for a while, just like we had before.

But would it even be possible with me in such a state?

What about Damien and his new relationship?

Or mine with Newt for that matter. I didn't want to give him up to go on the run for god's sake.

We could stay at the hospital for a time, but our enemies would catch us sooner or later.

On the opposite side of my hospital bed, a cot had been pulled into the room. Newt lay among the meager bedding, fast asleep. He'd gotten about as much rest as Damien, maybe less as he constantly hounded my doctors for information.

He was lucky to walk away so easily from the fight with the hospital administrator who tried to kill us. Cuts and bruises could have been much worse. The man wasn't a fighter. He'd gotten lucky, and only survived because his opponent wasn't a fighter either. If our enemies had sent a proper assassin after me that night, Newt wouldn't be alive now.

However, he was safe, and Madine Constella had been dragged off in handcuffs. She was being questioned by the FBI at that very moment. I didn't expect they would get much out of her, mostly because my opinion of the FBI was at an all time low, but it was a start.

Coin flip.

Heads: I'd walk again.

With the beeping of so many machines, and the noise of the hospital right outside my door, the room was never completely quiet. So, I didn't notice Newt waking up until his beautiful blue eyes were staring at me.

"Sebastian? You're awake. How are you? Do you need anything?"

The coin pressed into my palm, somehow still cool despite how much I'd been handling it.

"I should be asking you that. At this point, people have tried to kill you as many times as they've tried to kill me. How are you doing?"

My voice cracked like old paint—a combined symptom of smoke inhalation and having a breathing tube shoved down my throat during surgery—but Newt still smiled like it was the best sound he ever heard.

"I'm alive." He shrugged as he sat on

the edge of my bed. "And mostly uninjured. So, all in all, I can't complain."

He checked over my leg, making sure it was still hanging properly in its traction.

I'd seen the x-rays. While I'd been unconscious, doctors had opened up my leg and installed a bunch of pins to try and piece the limb back together. I couldn't remember how many pins, exactly, but the image made it look like my leg was more metal than bone.

I flipped the coin.

Tails: I'd never walk again.

"You should complain."

Newt froze in the middle of reading through my medical chart for the dozenth time.

"What?"

"You should complain. You should be furious at me for getting you involved in this. You shouldn't be here. If you left, then maybe they wouldn't—"

A finger pressed against my lips, silencing me. Newt snatched the coin from my hand, which I had been nervously flipping.

"Don't finish that sentence. You're about to suggest that we break up because it'll be safer for me, aren't you? I *am* furious. At this whole situation. Of course I am. But the people I'm mad at are the ones trying to kill us. Not you."

I tried to argue, but Newt's finger pressed firmer against my lips.

"Let me ask you this. If we claim to end our relationship and no longer have anything to do with each other, do you really think this 'Mafia Boss' guy will just believe that? He'll just leave me alone because you said so?"

The finger disappeared, but before I could answer, I was startled by the sound of laughter. At some point during our conversation, Damien had woken up, and now sat with an amused grin on his face, chuckling.

"Kid's got a point, Sebastian. You're a self-sacrificing idiot for no reason."

I grumbled but couldn't argue.

Newt ran a hand over my injured leg. His fingers were so light they barely made contact.

"Well, not always for nothing. Some of your sacrifices are very... noble. But in this case, no. I'm safer with you than apart from you. And it's where I want to be anyway. So no more suggesting that I leave. All right?"

"All right," I relented. There was no point arguing when Newt and Damien were both against me. I could barely hope to win an argument against one of them. Together they were an unstoppable force.

It would have been a perfect moment to kiss Newt. A lovely blush dusted over his cheeks, making his freckles stand out. However, I could barely raise my head off the pillows. The doctors had me pumped full of so many drugs, I felt nothing. I suppose I should have been grateful. Based on the extent of my injuries, I'd be in a lot of pain without the assistance of medication, but it also made me fuzzy in the head. My body refused to cooperate.

Instead, I settled for squeezing Newt's hand. It didn't require much movement, and based on the smile on Newt's face, he understood the message.

Even if I wished he could have stayed out of all this danger, I was also glad he was staying with me.

Our moment was interrupted when the door opened and Gabe stepped into the room, accompanied by a man I'd never seen. The man was definitely a Fed. Every person who worked for the FBI carried themselves with a certain confident set to their shoulders, and a stiffness to their movements, like they were always under scrutiny.

Damien stood from his chair, brushing out the wrinkles on his clothes and trying to smooth his beard into place.

"Director Thornton. What are you doing here, sir?"

While I didn't recognize the face, the name was familiar.

Willard Thornton. The director of the FBI.

Fuck.

Had we really earned such official attention?

Surely one private investigator getting blown up didn't warrant the director of the FBI getting personally involved.

I put on the best smile I could manage when I couldn't properly feel my face.

"Director? What an honor. I'd get up and shake your hand, but I think my nurse will actually tie me to the bed if I even try."

Out of the corner of my eye, I could see Damien glaring at me. It was a clear message that said, "Don't be an ass".

I'd never been very good at obeying directions.

Director Thornton stared at me for a moment. His gray eyes were flat, like he didn't know what to make of my flippant tone. But then a smile turned up the corners of his mouth.

"Mr. Roth. Your brother has mentioned your attitude before. I see he wasn't exaggerating."

It was my turn to shoot Damien a disgruntled look. I knew my brother maintained contact with the FBI, but when had he dealt with the director?

The FBI director took no notice of my silent conversation with Damien, or if he did, he chose to ignore it. "I'm glad to see these events haven't dampened your spirit. We're arranging protected accommodations for you as we speak. They should be ready soon so we can get you transferred."

Damien and I certainly had things to say about that, but surprisingly it was Newt who spoke up first. He shot to his feet, staring up at the director with hard blue eyes, despite being a whole head shorter than the other man.

"Sebastian can't go anywhere. It's important for his healing that he not be moved too much while the pins and stitches in his leg settle."

A sense of pride swelled in my chest as I watched Newt so fearlessly standing up to a man much bigger and more powerful than him. I shouldn't have been surprised. Newt was shy about a lot of things, but he had always been dedicated to his patients.

The director looked down at Newt, his smile still glued to his face. "Ah, the civilian nurse. Newton Clary, right? Not to worry, our people have been advised of the situation and will provide him with the care he needs."

Their people?

I didn't like the sound of that.

"Tell your people not to worry about me. I've already got a great nurse taking care of me."

Even in this tense situation, I couldn't help the softness that filled my eyes when I looked over at Newt.

In response, the director's smile grew stronger, turning his eyes into barely visible crescents. The only thing that kept the expression from looking like a snarl was the fact that his teeth weren't showing.

"I'm sure Mr. Clary has done well, but

he won't be needed any longer."

"Won't be needed?" Damien stepped protectively in front of Newt. "You make it sound like he won't be coming with us."

Watching my brother protect my boyfriend without a moment's hesitation should have brought a whole slew of warm emotions. Damien hadn't approved of most of my previous partners, mostly because I'd focused on quick hookups rather than actually dating. So, his easy acceptance of Newt was refreshing.

Unfortunately, it was tainted by the current situation.

The director's smile never wavered. "Witness protection is a means of preserving individuals that are important to an investigation. Mr. Clary will be sent home, and the two of you will be brought into our custody."

With one hand on Newt's shoulder, Damien shuffled him as far away from the director as the small room allowed. "That's not a good idea. We suspect the explosion at the apartment was an inside job. There's a traitor in your department, just like there was when Sebastian and I went into witness protection the first time. Gabe, tell him. You agreed with me when we talked about it earlier."

Until that moment, Gabe had stood like a quiet sentinel at the director's back, watching the exchange with sharp eyes. However, when Damien called out to him, his gaze locked onto the floor. His stance and posture never changed. His body may as well have been carved from marble, but the effort he put into avoiding eye contact spoke volumes.

"I do agree that it was likely an inside job."

His voice was even more stoic than usual. After living in the same apartment for weeks, we'd spent enough time together to no longer be strangers. While I still didn't know much about Gabe, we had at least been on casually good terms. Yet, it may as well have been my first meeting with the man, for he was even more rigid than usual.

After that one sentence, he fell silent and refused to say anymore.

"Yes, Agent Long has told me about the moments before the explosion. Tell me, Damien Roth, why did you insist on your brother going upstairs to the apartment while you stayed downstairs in the office? It's quite fortunate for you. Your brother nearly died, yet you walk away without a scratch.”

“I—” Damien stuttered. Damien never stuttered except for extreme circumstances.

This definitely qualified as extreme.

Despite all the pain meds I was on, a headache formed behind my eyes anyway.

We should have seen this coming.

Someone planting an explosive in an apartment under the FBI’s watch was too obvious to be ignored.

Either the FBI had to admit that they had a mole amongst their staff, or they had to find a patsy to take the fall.

If we weren’t careful, they could make my brother that patsy.

Damien was stunned into silence, but I scoffed and rolled my eyes. “Typical Fed assholes. I’m not surprised. Although, Gabe, I was actually starting to trust you. Guess I was wrong.”

Gabe still didn’t look at anyone or show any emotion at all. He was a statue in the shape of a man.

We could do nothing as the FBI barreled ahead with their plans to essentially kidnap us for their *witness protection* program. Damien couldn’t even argue for fear of being framed as a criminal. And I...

Well, I was useless.

If only I could walk, or at least stand up. We could have tried making a run for it like we did before. Damien and I had protected ourselves from David Russo's goons and corrupt FBI moles in the past. We could do it again.

But not with me in such a condition. Injured and bedridden, I was an anchor keeping my brother chained to the FBI's will.

For a moment, I considered suggesting that Damien should make a run for it without me, but I knew he'd never go for that idea.

If the situation were reversed, I wouldn't either.

Director Thornton made his excuses and left the room, leaving Gabe in charge of our relocation. I was transferred to a portable bed that could be wheeled out of the hospital, along with all the supplies and medication I would need.

My brother and I said nothing and just glared at Gabe silently as he directed other FBI agents to get the transport vehicles ready.

Newt, however, did continue to protest until Gabe relented and let him accompany us on the way out.

"To say goodbye," he claimed.

We made a glum parade, with Gabe leading the way, several FBI agents flanking us on either side, and Newt pushing my bed down the hospital hall.

I'd found another coin and flipped it over and over.

Heads: I'd walk again.

Tails: I'd never walk again.

I wanted to throw that bit of metal at Gabe's head, but doubted I'd be able to move my arm enough. Being transferred to a more portable bed, then wheeled down the hall, was testing the limits of my pain meds. Everything hurt and even small movements were difficult.

"You're a real fucker, you know that," I spat at the back of Gabe's head.

He didn't even bother to turn around and look at me. "You can think what you like about me, but you'll be grateful for our protection when you get out of this alive."

I laughed so hard I feared I'd snapped another rib.

"Survive? You think we're surviving

this? You're serving us up for Russo's people to kill at their leisure. This is a death march to the guillotine."

"They can try," Damien growled under his breath. "We'll see how many of their people I take down along the way."

He gripped something inside his pocket, and I knew he had a knife hidden within the lining of his coat, which he'd managed to sneak past hospital security. A single knife wouldn't fend off the entire FBI or Russo's henchmen, but we could at least make killing us a little harder for them.

At the end of the hall, we reached a set of elevators. There was limited space inside, especially with my transport bed. So, Gabe ushered Damien, Newt, and I through the doors and instructed the other FBI agents to meet us at the *Level 1* parking deck.

There was a slight bump as my bed rolled over the threshold of the elevator. I flinched as the jolt sent pain shooting up my leg, and the coin slipped from my fingers. I heard it hit the floor but didn't see where it landed.

Heads or Tails?

I'd never know.

SEBASTIAN

Newt was a flurry of activity, checking over the contraption strapped to my leg, and making sure all of my bandages and stitches were still in place. He tried to insist again that I shouldn't be moved, but Gabe ignored him and hit the button on the elevator panel.

The doors closed, sealing us inside the confined space. Once we were alone, Gabe sighed.

"We'll have to move fast. It won't take long for them to realize we're on the wrong floor." His hand landed gently on my shoulder. "I'm sorry, but we can't slow down for your comfort. You'll just have to endure it for a bit."

Confused, I looked to Damien to see if he knew what Gabe was talking about. However, Damien was busy staring intently at the elevator button panel.

The button for the *Level 3* parking deck was lit up. The hospital had three different parking decks, each one accessed by a different floor. Gabe had ordered the other FBI agents to the first parking deck, but that wasn't where we were headed.

The door chimed and opened before I could fully process what this meant.

"Come on," Gabe rushed us out of the elevator. "Move. We don't have long."

Newt and Damien together wheeled my bed off the elevator as fast as they dared. Every bump and jostle aggravated my wounds and had my nervous system lighting up like a malfunctioning Christmas tree.

I grit my teeth and dug my fingers into the sheets to try and ignore it.

The moment we stepped off the elevator, the sound of a honking horn greeted us. A large RV idled in the middle of the parking deck, and a familiar face waved at us from behind the wheel.

"Frankie?" Newt gaped as my bed was wheeled up next to the RV.

"Hey," Frankie waved again. "Come on. Get in. We're going... literally anywhere but here."

The RV had been chosen with care. Its side opened up into a handicap accessible lift. Usually intended for wheelchairs, it was large enough to lift my bed inside the RV with minimal jostling.

It was a big RV and would have been considered spacious if it weren't trying to contain my wheeled bed along with four other grown men. There was just enough seating for everyone, so long as Frankie stayed behind the wheel.

As soon as everyone was inside, Frankie put the RV into drive and started maneuvering it through the maze of the parking deck.

"Do you know how to drive this thing?" I asked as he came precariously close to hitting one of the parking deck's support columns.

"My parents had an RV. They taught me how to drive it, but that was a long time ago and theirs wasn't as big as this. Don't worry, though. I've got it handled."

Though there were a few close calls, we did manage to make it out of the parking deck. Once we were driving smoothly down the road, I breathed a sigh of relief.

Newt was still checking over my injuries, but I didn't hurt so much now that my bed was stationary. Instead, I turned my attention to Damien and Gabe, who sat across from each other at the RV's bench table.

"Why are you helping us?" Damien asked Gabe, the scowl still etched on his face. "You just defied your director's orders. You'll lose your job over this."

Gabe leaned forward until his elbows

rested on the table. It was an odd sight. I hadn't realized the man's spine could bend enough to slouch.

"Because you're right," he said. "Until we know who the mole inside our agency is, taking you into witness protection is basically the same as handing you over to be executed. Also, you're not the only one who wants to see the David Russo taken out."

He gestured down at the table, where a laptop and stacks of folders sat. It seemed to be a copy of all the info we'd managed to find about David Russo and the Mariano family, the missing children, and the pedophile ring.

"We've got a tangled web to unwind here."

Gabe pulled out his glasses from the inner pocket of his jacket and perched them on his nose.

"So, let's get to work."

Dear Reader,

Thank you for reading Sebastian & Newt's story. You may have remembered Newt from the Smokejumpers series, where he spends his days as an ambulance driver for Station Twenty-One. Who knew he moonlighted as a nurse too! Busy boy.

Sebastian seems to have taken his time deciding on who he wanted to woo, and how to tie up so many other loose ends in the series (and possibly other series too!), but he's at least started us off. Finally.

While we've successfully brought these boys together in this book, with them happy for now at least, they annoyingly decided the story arc needed to continue. Yeah, a bit of a cliffy. Blame them, not me! I'm just the messenger. Lol.

So, on that note, Gabe is going to take the lead, starting with his outright defiance of the FBI Director and whisking Damien, Sebastian, Newt, and Frankie off to parts unknown under his protection. Can I just say I'm kind of glad it turned out that Gabe was on Damien and Sebastian's side in all this? Good man to have in their corner, I think. For a minute there I started to wonder if he'd turned on them too. Whew.

Oh, and as per my usual, you may have found a few breadcrumbs between the pages. Have no fear, those stories are to come.

As for what the FBI and FPA are currently calling the CAP group, that's a nod to an amazing author, E.M. Leya, whose Save The Kids series actually inspired me to write the Federal Protection Agency series. You can read the first book in her series, Pain, available at your favorite online retailer.

Anyway, clickity-click to continue the story with Gabe, book eight in the Federal Protection Agency Series!

OTHER BOOKS BY EVIE

Federal Protection Agency
Mason
Rafe
Ryzen
Cooper
Noah
Damien
Sebastian
Gabe
Logan

Ruthless Empire
Courting Danger
Chasing Danger
Kissing Danger

Smokejumpers
Hawke
Cyrus
Jase
Gage
Jackson
Xavier

EVIE RILEY

Jasper Springs
Cade
Dawson
Drew
Grayson
Riley
Mitch

From The Edge
Shattered
Runaway
Jaded
Rescue
Hidden
Tormented

Gray Vale Pack
His Fated Mate
His Wounded Warrior
His Healing Heart

ABOUT THE AUTHOR

Evie Riley is a prolific, neurodivergent author known for her captivating MM romance novels. She has gained a significant following and topped the LGBT+ action and adventure bestseller charts with her series.

Evie's writing style often explores dark and gritty themes where her men must overcome difficult obstacles in their search for love, but she has also ventured into sweeter small-town romances, incorporating tropes like enemies-to-lovers, friends-to-lovers, age-gap, and forced proximity. She is known for crafting engaging romantic suspense novels and has a knack for creating interconnected series worlds that keep readers invested.

EVIE RILEY

Interestingly, Ms. Riley has hinted at exploring new genres, such as Alien Omegaverse Romance, in the future.

Outside of writing, she enjoys spending time at the beach and has a quirky personality, described by her partner as ranging from cute to deadly, depending on her blood-chocolate levels.

Evie spends her nights writing bad boys in love, and her days wrangling the sweet boys she loves.